The Following

ISLA GREEN

Copyright © 2023 Isla Green

All rights reserved.

ISBN: 9798375381800

To J and A,
With love

ACKNOWLEDGMENTS

WITH THANKS TO JS, for your conversations, copious draft reading and belief in me and the book.

TO NJ, for your thoughts, inspiration and for being there with me.

TO JH, for sharing our experiences and the deconstruction process.

One

The church

'I have something grave to tell you.' Pastor Loveday grips onto the lectern with both hands, his expression sombre. Crisp April sunlight radiates through the arched museum windows onto his thinning grey hair, the familiar navy blue suit.

Sam, along with the other five hundred members of the congregation, watches her father intently. His usually pallid complexion is rather pink.

The church has been convening here in Bristol City Museum for the past six months. Before that, they rented the dusty assembly hall of a shabby secondary school in Fishponds. The museum hall, with its stone pillars, towering ceilings and dark, theatrical paintings, is a gift from God. This is the beacon from which God will fill the city with his light.

'It has become known to us that a member of our congregation, John Fisher, has recently departed from his wife and family.' Her father pauses. 'He has made a wilful choice to live in sin with another of our members, Marilyn Peters.'

There is whispering along the back row, where most of the young people sit each Sunday morning. Sam glances at Greta beside her; her friend raises her eyebrows. Who would have thought it? Quiet, sensible John with sexy Marilyn Peters, and without any of them noticing. She can't recall when she last saw either John or Marilyn.

'This is a particularly sad occasion for those of you who've worked closely with John. As you know, John and Rachel have led the youth group for a number of years.'

That must be why the youth meetings have been cancelled, although her parents have said nothing in front of her. Being the pastor's daughter frequently means she finds out news before other church members, and knowing things that are best left unspoken about, like the time when Eileen Anderson, who had an obsession with her father, lay on their front lawn all night, refusing to get up. They'd had to call the police in the end. Her mother said that Eileen couldn't help it: she had mental health problems.

'Adultery is a sin in the eyes of the Lord,' Pastor Loveday

continues, steadily. 'I hereby announce, on behalf of the church leadership, that John Fisher and Marilyn Peters have forfeited their right to remain members of this congregation. I ask you to all please remember Rachel Fisher and her two young children. Let us bow our heads in prayer.'

Sam closes her eyelids to an image of John and Marilyn in a swirl of red light and naked bodies. She hastily opens them again, glimpsing Joe, seated in the row of musicians at the side of the stage, handsome with his white t-shirt and gelled blond hair, his sleek white bass guitar propped up behind him.

'I have something else important to announce this morning.' The pastor's demeanour has transformed into his more commonly cheerful self. 'I have the pleasure of introducing two newcomers into our fellowship: the Reverend Kurt West and his wife, Francesca.' He motions towards the front row. 'I'd like to give them a warm welcome into our family.'

The couple stand, stepping up to the platform beside her father. The new minister isn't anything like the other church leaders: his short-sleeved shirt emphasises bulging muscular arms. His wife is wearing an elegant, olive green dress.

'Kurt and Francesca have come to us all the way from a church in California. God has called them on a mission to England, specifically to work with our young people.' The pastor unhooks the microphone, handing it to Kurt.

'Thank you.' Kurt beams, his white teeth sparkling in contrast to his tan. 'It's a great honour to be here this morning to carry out God's work. God has exciting plans!' He raises his voice, dynamically. 'God has sent me here for a purpose! To shake up the youth in this country!'

'Is Joe coming?' Greta pulls on her denim jacket.

Sam scans the museum: the congregation have now dispersed around the hall and into the foyer, milling, chatting and laughing. 'Doesn't look like it.'

They slip out through the glass porch, across the street to Castle Park, where couples have camped out on the grass, under the iron bridge by St Peter's church and down the stone steps to the towpath. On the other side of the murky canal the buildings are derelict, their walls blackened and windows smashed. The path here is secluded, the ground littered with a spilt bag of chips, crushed lager cans and cigarette butts.

They perch on the chipped, damp edge of one of the benches. Greta pulls out a packet of Embassy No 1 and her silver Zippo from her jacket pocket. 'What about John Fisher and Marilyn Peters, then? I mean, she's the most stylish woman in church. Can you imagine her and John…?'

'I know. I can't.' She accepts a cigarette, props it between her middle and forefinger.

Greta flicks open the Zippo, lights first Sam's cigarette and then her own. 'And that new couple this morning…'

Sam holds the lit end at arm's length to prevent her Monsoon dress from absorbing the scent of smoke. 'I haven't told you about Joe yet, have I?'

'What's he done?'

'It's just him and that Kurt guy.'

'The preacher?'

'Joe won't stop talking about him - they're staying at his house. On the phone every night it's Kurt this, Kurt that. He used to be a stunt man and a karate champion - can you believe that? And Francesca won Miss America last year.'

'Wow! Did she? She's attractive, don't you think?'

'I s'pose. My dad's gone and invited them for Sunday dinner,' she moans. 'Joe's coming, so he's ecstatic.'

Two

Calling

Kurt clasps hold of Joe's hand to his left, Francesca's to his right, signalling that the others at the table should join together also: a ritual that is new to their family.

They are squeezed around the narrow pine table: Sam on the stool between her father and sister, Stella; her mother, Joe, Kurt and Francesca opposite. Their shoulders are hunched together, the dining table even more cramped now with their hands linked.

Kurt closes his eyes, waits while everyone follows. 'Lord, we thank you for bringing each of us here today to share together around this table. We thank you for the wonderful food you have provided for us. Amen.'

As she opens her eyes, her mother smiles around the table. 'I'll just fetch the gravy.'

'Anyone else for more potatoes?' Her mother scoops second helpings of roast potatoes onto Kurt's plate, then Joe's. 'Sam?'

'You're joking! I'll burst!'

'She's so cute!' Kurt swallows another mouthful of chicken and nudges Joe with his elbow.

'Kurt!' Francesca casts him a mock, cross look. 'Leave her alone.' She smiles at Sam across the table. 'I'm sorry. Don't mind him: he's always embarrassing people. He enjoys it.'

'It's fine.' She meets the woman's eyes, awkwardly. 'I like the colour of your dress.'

'Thank you. I had it designed by my dressmaker in America.'

Sam gazes down at her plate.

'Is this your first visit to Bristol?' asks Stella, who has been unusually quiet throughout the meal.

Francesca nods, 'I've never been to England before.'

'Tell everyone the story about how you died and came back to life,' Joe interrupts, grinning widely at Kurt.

'Well…' Kurt beams. 'I used to be a stuntman in the days before I found God.' He places his knife and fork together on his plate. 'I'd been doing a dangerous stunt from the top of a skyscraper - the usual sort of thing - when something went wrong with the safety equipment. Suddenly, I was falling thousands of feet to my death.'

Everyone stares at Kurt, transfixed.

'When I was lying dead on the ground, an angel appeared and carried me to heaven. I looked down at my empty body on earth and it was then that I knew what I had to do.' He pauses, making eye contact with each of them around the table, his eyes blazing. 'God was calling me on a mission to set the world on fire.'

'That's so fantastic!' Joe says, even though he's obviously heard the story before.

Kurt gives him a manly pat on the back, continuing, 'I returned to my body and there I was, alive again! The film crew and the other stunt guys were totally amazed. Soon after that, of course, I became a preacher.'

Stella stands, gathering the dinner plates. 'Who would like lemon meringue pie?'

'Can you hold on?' Kurt flashes her a smile. 'The best part is just coming.'

'I'll move these out the way.' Stella is already heading towards the door.

Sam slips out from her place on the stool and follows her into the kitchen.

Her sister unlatches the steamed-up window, pushes the backdoor open - 'Go on, Henry' – and the cat shoots out into the garden.

'That man hasn't stopped talking!' Sam starts to giggle.

Stella stands for a moment by the open door. 'He's quite unbelievable!' She rubs her forehead, closing her eyes.

'We could escape before they notice.'

'Don't! Or I won't be able to go back in. There,' Stella waves her hand towards the worktop, 'you take the dishes and cream.'

Kurt is launching into the second part of his story: 'God had given me one miracle, but little did I know he was about to give me a second.'

Stella portions the lemon meringue pie into the bowls, passing them along the table.

'I picked up the newspaper one day and on the front page was a photograph of Francesca. I'd never met her at this point. Her picture was in all the papers because she'd won Miss America, which, as you all know, is the most prestigious beauty contest in the world. I knew, in that moment, this was the woman God intended to be my wife.'

All eyes fix on Francesca.

'But there was one small problem: she was the other side of America!' He laughs, heartily.

Francesca takes his hand on the tablecloth, her tanned fingers entwining with his.

'So I raced to the airport, caught the next available flight to New York and we got married straight away. Then God called us to England… but I'll leave the rest for tonight.'

'Tonight?' Stella asks, spooning the last scoop of meringue into her dish.

'Kurt's speaking in the service.' Her father smiles warmly at his guest.

It's all right for her sister, Sam thinks: she never comes to the meetings anyway.

'I'm going now,' Sam calls from the hallway. Joe is still in the front room, listening to Kurt.

He runs to catch up with her at the corner of Trenchard Street, his baseball jacket slung over his shoulder. 'What's the hurry?'

'You're so slow! I've been waiting ages.'

'I was talking. They're interesting, aren't they?'

'Are they?'

'You thought so too. I could tell.'

'You don't know everything. I thought they were a bit over the top.'

'Just because Kurt isn't boring and ordinary, like everyone else. He's-'

'Let's just leave it.'

They walk up Old Church Road towards the path that leads through the woods.

Joe reaches to hold her hand. 'Kurt said you look like her.'

'Like who?'

'Who do you think? Francesca.'

'Yeah, right! He's never seen me before so he can't have said that.'

'He did. In the service, when I pointed you out.'

Once they're hidden by the trees, Joe fumbles for the gold Benson & Hedges packet in his pocket. He takes out a cigarette, offering one to Sam.

'Thanks.'

At the top of Church Hill, they stop to sit on the bench overlooking the estuary. His kiss tastes of cold air, tobacco and Polo mints.

Henry is rubbing against her legs; his food bowl is empty. There's a yellow Post-it stuck to the kitchen table beside a plate of cheese rolls and two slices of Victoria Sponge Cake.

Sam unpeels the note. 'I'm taking Stella home. Dad gone to Winstanley's with Kurt and Francesca. Mum x.' She feels oddly disappointed.

Joe unpacks his sports bag in her bedroom: hair gel, comb, Brut aftershave, toothbrush, a neatly folded, pale blue t-shirt.

'I've eaten too much!' She holds her stomach.

He smirks. 'That's nothing! I ate a whole Victoria Sponge Cake once.'

She puts on the same green dress that she wore to the morning service; the Indian cotton is light against her skin. Joe is always going on at her to dress like the other girls at church, in glitzy blouses, figure hugging skirts and stilettos, their faces carefully made up, hair curled, flicked and sprayed in place. Avril gave her some of her old make-up but it makes her look all wrong.

She can hear Joe in the bathroom, brushing his teeth. She squirts Panache onto her neck and wrists and stands in front of the mirror. If only she could look sophisticated, she thinks, like Francesca.

'Go and ask her to sit with us.' Greta nods towards Francesca, standing at the back of the hall.

'I can't do that!'

'Yes, you can! Go on! Look, she's got no-one to sit with.'

Sam scans the hall: Joe's at the front with the musicians, laughing about something with Lucy Longthorn; her father has disappeared into the crypt with Kurt and the Ministry Team, to pray before the service. Kurt will be sitting on the platform tonight with the elders. Francesca is standing alone, gazing at the rows of chairs as they fill with people. 'What shall I say? I don't even know her.'

'You met her at lunchtime. Go on, then! I'll come with you.'

'Okay.' Hesitantly, she approaches the woman.

Francesca turns. 'Hi there!'

'This is my friend, Greta.'

Greta grins. 'There's a spare seat next to us, if you like. Over there.' She gestures towards the back row.

'That's nice. Thanks, guys.'

'Good evening, and a warm welcome to you all tonight.' Pastor Loveday smiles out across the gathering. 'Before we begin, I'd like you all to turn and greet those around you. Bless your neighbour with the love of God!'

The hall erupts with noise as members of the congregation stand, hugging, kissing, making animated conversation. Sam glances in Francesca's direction, two seats along: Nick, smartly turned out tonight in a navy blue pinstripe suit, is shaking her hand.

She's about to follow Greta into the foyer when Betty Evans leans across the chairs, squeezing her into a breathtaking hug. 'May God bless you, my dear.'

She forces a smile. 'Thank you.'

The band strikes up, Megan Morris, the keyboard player, singing into the microphone, '*Link us as one, Lord…*'

The rest of the assembly join in: '*Link us as one with bonds that cannot be severed; link us as one, Lord, link us as one. Link us as one with love.*'

Megan sings the verses, passionately: '*You are the children of God, you are the heavenly wine, you are his elected ones, you are the glorious divine…,*' the gathering joining in with the chorus: '*Link us as one…*'

The musicians switch to a lively song and the congregation leap to their feet, clapping hands, arms raised in praise, the black women swinging their tambourines in the aisles; '*I'm creating a nation of power, a following of praise, who will travel this land with my Spirit…*'

'Lord, I pray for anyone here who has not yet given their lives to you.' Pastor Loveday speaks quietly into the microphone. 'I ask that you will call them to you tonight, so that they might know your loving kindness and grace... I'd like to ask anyone who God is calling to pray in your heads with me now, 'Father, I have sinned against Heaven. I have yielded to the world, the flesh, the Devil. Have mercy on me."

The museum hall is silent. All heads are bowed.

'If you have made that step this evening, or if you have already given your heart to God and you'd like to receive more of his healing spirit, can I ask you to come forward to stand in front of the platform here and the leaders will pray with you.'

The musicians play softly and the congregation sing quietly as people move to the front. Sam senses Francesca rise from her seat and make her way along the royal blue carpet down the centre aisle, joining Kurt in front of the stage. The other leaders are already moving from person to person, praying.

The new couple approach a young man standing alone with his head lowered. Kurt steps behind, Francesca in front; laying hands on him, they begin praying aloud, mouths moving in unison. The young man wavers for a moment; Kurt breaks his fall, lowering him gently to the floor.

Three

Truth

'Get out!' Mrs Twist screeches at Greta across the hall, her cheeks puffing fiercely, her triple chin trembling. 'Go and stand outside my office!'

The heads of the entire fifth year swivel around to stare at Sam and Greta, in the back corner of the assembly room.

Mrs Twist has just finished Monday morning assembly, where she conducted them all singing 'To be a pilgrim' and delivered a lecture on the importance of knuckling down to hard work: 'Your GCSE exams are approaching, Year Five. You are reaching the most important point in your school lives.'

Mrs Twist dishes out two detentions: the first because of the red t-shirt (spotted across the assembly hall) poking out of Greta's white school blouse, and the second because Greta has just laughed. This means that she receives the ultimate detention, the punishment administered when anyone receives two lunchtime detentions in the same week: tonight, after school, in the sixth form block with the rough boys.

'I can see a word written on your forehead,' she tells Greta, in front of Sam, Mrs Cadenhead, Mr Pike and a group of gawping second years on their way to first lesson. 'It spells failure! Nobody would think you were at the top of the senior school, about to take your GCSE's. You're a complete waste of time!'

Mr Allen's briefcase is perched, as usual, on top of the teacher's desk by the blackboard. He is leaning against the window ledge reading from 'The Catcher in the Rye', his voice throaty, Adam's apple bobbing up and down. This morning he is wearing his grey cords and grey flecked shirt.

'Okay, folks, I'd like you to look back over the last chapter and discuss the questions on the board. Work in pairs, please, and make notes on your ideas. While you're doing that, I'll be coming round to collect your creative extensions.'

Last week, Mr Allen set the class to write a coursework assignment on 'The Catcher in the Rye', continuing the story in the voice of the protagonist, Holden, who says words like 'fuck' and 'Jesus Christ' in every sentence. Sam enjoyed writing the piece using all the forbidden words. Julia Lamb and Cary Bell went whining to their parents to write letters of complaint to the school. Mr Allen has set Julia and Cary another essay, writing in the voice of Holden's sister, Phoebe, who doesn't swear at all.

'How're we doing over here?' Mr Allen glances, good-humouredly, from Sam to Greta. He knows she and Greta chat in lessons but he doesn't mind.

Greta reciprocates with her most flirtatious smile.

The colour rises in his neck: he's easily embarrassed.

'Is it still okay for me to come round tonight?' Sam whispers, when he's moved to Julia and Cary's table.

'Yeah, Mum's out, so we'll have the place to ourselves. Come round as early as you can.'

'Okay. Joe's helping Kurt and Francesca move all weekend.'

'Oh God!' Greta grimaces. 'Why don't we go into Bristol on Saturday? Top Gun's on in Whiteladies Road. With Tom Cruise!'

'A whole hour writing stupid lines!' Greta yanks her denim jacket from her locker. 'Mrs Twist said she might not let me into the sixth form. I'll have to redo the fifth year.'

'She just enjoys winding people up.'

'Yeah, well I'm not staying on at school, anyway.'

'What about your A levels? Mr Allen said you should definitely take English.'

Greta shakes her head. 'As soon as the exams are over, I'm never coming anywhere near this place again.' She slings her jacket over her shoulder, heading down the corridor. 'See you later.'

Sam opens her locker, removes her stonewash denim jacket and shoves her armful of books and folders inside. She peers out of the window overlooking the staff car park, just in time to catch sight of Mr Allen stepping through the main entrance. She and Greta hang about here every day until quarter to four to observe this occurrence; it never fails to make them laugh. Today, though, watching alone by the window, she feels conspicuous. His familiar figure, adorned in the grey cords and carrying the brown leather briefcase, strolls across the car park; he unlocks the door to his Fiesta and disappears inside. She watches the green car reverse and drive slowly around the side of the school building.

She wanders along the first floor corridor, past the French rooms, the history rooms. The place is deserted already; even the teachers have packed up and gone for the weekend. Greta will hate staying here until five.

Greta runs her fingers along the stack of cassettes beside the stereo. 'What d'you want to listen to?'

'I don't know. You choose something.'

Greta's house, a five-storey Victorian terrace on Clevedon sea front, is much more interesting than Sam's ordinary estate house. Greta's parents bought the house before they split up. It has no central heating; curtains and doors are missing; the floorboards are jagged and spiked with nails; the walls are textured with years of multi-coloured flaking layers of paint.

A gravelly voice sounds from the speakers. 'Bob Dylan,' Greta grins. 'I'll get some ice.'

'Come and sit down.' Sam is holding her half-filled glass. 'Let me taste it first.'

Greta kneels on the faded Persian rug and picks up the Malibu bottle. She fills up her own glass to the brim.

'That's nearly the whole bottle! Are you sure your mum won't mind?' Lou, Greta's mother, is at work, singing in a pub.

'It was a present. Mum says it's too sweet.'

She lifts her drink to her mouth. 'Ughh! It's disgusting! I can't...'

Greta takes her glass and rapidly swallows the clear liquid, then twists away, her hand pressed over her mouth.

'How d'you feel?'

Both glasses empty, Sam is flat on her back, clutching her stomach. 'Stop it! Stop making me laugh!'

Greta crawls out of the room on hands and knees.

Her eyes are streaming; she can hear her friend spluttering over the rattle of the harmonica.

'Let's go outside,' Greta calls from the hallway.

She pulls herself to her feet, wobbles past the ginger kittens that are slipping and skidding on the tiled hallway floor.

Greta ushers her through the front door, across the road to the wooden jetty. Red and blue fishing boats bob on the surface of the water. Behind them, the promenade and the terrace of houses are wonky. She has to lie down, propping herself up with her elbow. 'Let's play Truth.'

They had been playing it earlier in Home Economics; Greta spent the whole lesson trying to glean from Sam her top three people. She had finally given her answer: Greta, Mr Allen and Joe - although, if she's entirely honest, Joe would be more like number four or five.

'It's my turn.' She tries to think of a new question. 'Mm… Is there anything no-one knows about you?'

'There might be.'

'Not allowed! You have to answer.'

Greta flips onto her stomach; she lowers her arm to drape over the side of the jetty, dragging her fingers through the water. 'It's nothing. There isn't anything.'

It's growing darker. Further along on the beach, the group of boys playing football are out of focus in the dimming light.

'What's that in your hand?' She scoops the water beside Greta's hand. Her palms, in the dusk, fill with tiny sparks, disappearing through her fingers. 'What is it?'

'Phosphorescence. Mum told me.'

She slides closer to the edge of the jetty; hundreds of tiny dots glow in the dark water.

'Let's go swimming!' Greta is already picking her way over the rocks to the beach.

'What, now?' she calls after her. 'The sea's freezing!'

Greta unbuttons her shirt and jeans, dropping them in a pile at her feet. She's in the water in seconds, her head ducking under the black waves; several strong strokes and she's out past the rocks. She turns, treading water. 'Come on!'

Sam slowly unpeels her clothes, down to her white cotton underwear. As she wades into the sea, lights spark off her knees and thighs. She holds her breath as the cold liquid covers her stomach. She can just make out Greta's shadowy head by the red fishing boat, way out past the end of the jetty.

Four

Power

Sam unzips the bag of discarded make-up given to her by Avril after the Sunday evening service a few weeks ago. Pressing as close as she can to the dressing table mirror, she outlines her eyes with Special Eyes dark brown eyeliner and curls her eyelashes with Endless Lash mascara.

She pulls out a red t-shirt from her wardrobe, immediately flinging it onto the carpet with the other garments. She's been trying on outfits for the past hour. She badly needs some new clothes, she thinks; her old things that her mother bought her, from Etam and Topgirl, are too bright, too childish.

'Are you ready?' her mother asks, as Sam dashes past her into the dining room.

'Nearly. I just need to ring Greta.'

'But you're picking her up soon! And you've had all day to-'

'I'll be quick.' She holds the receiver to her ear and dials her friend's number. 'It's me.'

'Oh hi!'

'Have you packed yet?'

'Almost. It's just a night - we don't need much.'

'I don't know what to wear.'

'Jeans and a t-shirt: it's only casual.'

'But which jeans and which t-shirt?'

'Erm... those jeans with shells and beads sewn into the waist, and your long-sleeved turquoise t-shirt.'

'Thanks. See you in a few minutes. Don't forget your sleeping bag!'

In her room, she hastily retrieves the selected items from the pile on the floor and slips on her gold hooped earrings.

'Sam!' her mother calls, impatiently. 'Dad's waiting in the car!'

'Okay, guys,' Kurt commences the meeting, 'I'm told you've been having a few problems. Well, we're here to get you all moving.'

Sam glances around the group of young people, sitting quietly in the circle of red plastic chairs. Fifteen or so of the usual crowd have turned up. Joe has acquired a new baseball hat, she notices, similar to Kurt's, and has swung the cap around to face the back, the way Kurt wears it.

'It's my belief,' the preacher leans forward in his seat, 'that God wants to use *you*, the youth, to change the church. God wants to shake you up! He wants to give you new powers!'

He stands, motioning for the group to join him. 'Let's give God our praises together.'

Joe picks up his acoustic guitar and begins playing 'Holy Father', his eyes closed, face animated.

Everyone follows: '*How did I live without your fatherhood and tender care?*'

She hasn't had chance to speak to Joe since they arrived. She hasn't seen him on his own for two weeks and now here he is, leading the worship.

'*I will praise you, I will praise you, I will praise you forever…*'

Kurt's arms are stretched out, dramatically; beside him, Francesca stands serenely, her eyes closed, her palms raised upwards. She's wearing an amazing pair of jeans and boots, Sam thinks, trying not to stare at her across the room.

Greta, next to her, is mute, her eyes cast down towards the floor, causing Sam to feel like abstaining also.

'*I have no shame, no more do I stand in blame, here in God's grace…*'

Kurt dances, joined by Pippa and Sarah. Even Joe is half-dancing, his movement hindered by the guitar strapped around his neck. He slows the rhythm, indicating the last round of the chorus. Gradually, they are seated and the room grows still.

'Lord, I ask that you will come down and move among us this evening!' Kurt prays, dynamically. 'I ask that these young people will be open to all the power you want to give them. Amen.'

Pippa's voice fills the silence: 'Jesus, I love you above anything else. I want to carry out your will in everything I do.'

Kurt prays aloud, suddenly, in tongues, his face tense and passionate; people are chanting in tongues. She presses her arms tightly to her chest as the Spirit moves around the room.

'God is saying to all of us that he wants us to give up everything *now* and begin the work he has planned for us.' Her eyes snap open at Joe's voice; his eyes are closed as though his words are being channelled from another place. 'There's so little time! We have to take the power that is given to us, *now*! We're going to do great things! We're going to change the world!'

'What's he like!' Greta mutters under her breath, rolling her eyes towards Joe. 'Look, he's still carrying his bloody Bible.'

She glances towards the back of Joe's white t-shirt; he's talking about something with Kurt, in a hushed voice, as the others trail into the kitchen to make tea and coffee. Greta probably hasn't even got a Bible, she thinks; she's never seen her with one.

'What's happened to being in a band?' Greta scowls. 'And writing songs? Bono?'

'He still likes U2, I think.'

'You see! You're not sure, are you? Coming for a cig?'

She shakes her head.

'Suit yourself. I'll go on my own then!' Greta saunters off.

Francesca is standing alone by the kitchen window; she could go over and talk to her, Sam thinks. Sensing herself grow flustered, she heads, instead, for Joe.

He leans towards her, his face glowing. 'I'm praying for Greta.'

'I can never sleep in a room with other people,' Avril's well-spoken voice resonates from one of the bumps in the darkness, 'but I tell myself it's doing me good just to lie here resting.'

Avril doesn't go to Clevedon High School with Sam and the other younger girls. She attends Coulston's, a private day school in the city centre. In the chilly ladies' toilets, where they all brushed their teeth and changed for bed, Avril had adorned herself in a pair of Calvin Klein pinstriped pyjamas and applied another coat of red lipstick, before making an appearance in front of the boys in the museum hall.

The girls have been allocated the left side of the hall and the boys the right, sleeping bags spread out across the matted blue carpet. Avril is the only one who's had the foresight to bring a sleeping mat. Sam is lying beside Greta under a painting of the disciples being baptised by fire on the Day of Pentecost, on top of her sleeping bag to provide extra cushioning. She can only lie on her side for a few minutes before her arm goes dead.

'Did you see what the morning meeting's about?' Greta whispers. 'On the flipchart?'

Since Robin and Pippa's team-building games before bedtime,

she's forgotten about the meetings. 'No, what?'

'Sex.' Greta giggles, noisily.

She focuses on keeping every muscle in her body perfectly still. The inside of her eyelids are red, her hands clammy.

'In the Bible, it's written that fornication is a sin,' Kurt tells them. 'I want you to close your eyes now and seek God's message to each of you about your sexuality.'

She catches the faint whiff of tobacco from Greta in the neighbouring seat.

'God is saying there's someone in this room right now who is committing sins of the flesh...'

She holds her breathe. She daren't open her eyes in case Kurt is watching her.

'He wants you to ask for forgiveness this afternoon and seek the cleansing of the Holy Spirit.'

Are sins of the flesh fornication, she wonders? Whatever *that* is. Does what she and Joe have done come into that category? She thought it didn't count as sex, but maybe it was fornication. She'll talk to Greta about it later. If it *is* a sin, then Pippa and Robin are sinning too: Joe told her they do everything except go all the way.

Joe is deep in conversation with Francesca. She looks so classy in that charcoal shirt, Sam thinks, with the jeans she had on yesterday. What are the two of them talking about? They keep laughing. It's obvious Joe's attracted to her.

'Is that all the break we're getting?' Greta moans, as they take their seats in the meeting room again. Her blonde fringe is sticking up in tufts where she keeps running her fingers through it. 'I hate orange juice!'

'You didn't have to have it! It's supper after this.'

'It's unhealthy, being stuck in a dark building all day. We haven't breathed in any real air since yesterday.'

'*You* have,' she whispers. 'Don't go out again you, will you? Someone will notice.'

'Those of you who heard my sermon last Sunday will know how important I feel this subject is.' Kurt's piercing eyes scan the circle. 'God has given us the power to heal! In the Bible, when the disciples prayed, all those who were sick became well again.' He raises his voice.

'It's God's will that *all* shall be healed!'

She looks down at her baseball boots, poking from the legs of her jeans.

'If any who are sick are not healed, then *we* are to be held accountable! Our faith isn't strong enough! We're not believing! God has given us the power to heal and he demands that we use it *now*!' His eyes blaze, his body poised, as though he's about to spring out of the chair. 'God is saying that *all* shall be healed!'

'My dad *does* believe!' Ben cries out, suddenly.

All heads in the group turns to stare at him. Ben Goodman is a tall, skinny boy, with bad skin. He used to give Sam and Greta lifts to the youth meetings in his black MG Convertible before he moved into the city; he always put the roof down, even in winter.

His face grows red, screws up and he breaks into sobbing.

No-one says anything. Ben's father, Tim, stands in the museum foyer every Sunday, heartily shaking the hands of church members as they arrive. Everyone knows he has a terminal illness; *he* hasn't been healed.

It's too late, Sam thinks, miserably. The evening meeting is almost finished, the residential coming to an end, and things have happened to everyone except her. Was Joe speaking in tongues? She thought she heard him. Some of the others definitely were. She has never been able to; she's *tried*, in the church services, at youth events, on summer camp, but it's never worked. She can't even pray in her head without becoming distracted.

'If there are any of you here who haven't yet been filled with God's spirit and you want him to touch you tonight,' Kurt addresses the circle, sitting silently with their eyes closed, 'can you signal now by raising your hand.'

Pushing Greta and Joe from her awareness, she lifts her hand.

'Thank you. I'd like you to stand so that we can pray with you.'

Others are standing also: Sarah, Nick, Maria. The rest of the group moves around them.

She feels strange, light-headed. Francesca is walking across the room towards her, smiling, placing her hands on her shoulders. She closes her eyes.

Francesca speaks in tongues; a murmuring spreads through the room as others pray aloud. Her skin, under her t-shirt, is warm beneath

Francesca's palms; something is brushing against her arms and back, pressing down on her head. Everything is dimming…

When she opens her eyes, she's lying on the floor, enveloped in warmth and light.

Five

Union

Sam begins organising the shopping onto the shelves in the fridge: Dairy Lee cheese triangles, chocolate Penguin biscuits.

'Thanks, love.' Her mother places the last armful of Tesco's carrier bags from the car onto the breakfast table.

The telephone is ringing. 'I'll get it.' She drops the box of Weetabix and dashes into the other room. 'It's probably Greta.'

She picks up the receiver: 'Hello?'

'Sam!' Joe's voice says, jovially.

'Oh... hi.'

'D'you want to do something today?'

She hesitates. 'I can't really... I've said I'll go to the flea market with Greta.'

'The flea market?'

'You know - in St Nicholas - where I took you at Christmas.'

'But what about seeing *me*? You always see me on Saturdays.'

'I don't. We haven't done anything for weeks.'

'Oh *great*! A couple of important things come up, and you've forgotten about me already!'

'Of course I haven't!'

'Are we meeting today then?'

'I promised Greta-'

'Thanks a lot! You see Greta every day at school. What about me?'

Holding the receiver to her ear, she stretches the telephone cord across to the window, undoing the catch and pushing it ajar. Her father is sitting in a deckchair on the patio, immersed in a book.

'I don't *believe* you!' Joe huffs.

Through the open window, she watches her mother carry out a mug of tea and a slice of Battenburg cake for her father.

'So are we gonna meet then? Come on...'

'Well, maybe I-'

'I've got a surprise for you.'

'What?'

'I'll tell you when I see you.' He sounds pleased with himself.

'Well, okay then...'
'The usual place? One o'clock?'
'Okay.'
'Great.' His voice sounds cheerful again. 'You're wonderful! See you later.'
'See you.' She presses the disconnect button and frowns, dialling Greta's number.

She glances up at the hands of the bus station clock: it's only twelve o'clock. In the Haymarket underpass, a scruffy-looking man with a guitar is singing out of tune; he stops playing, removes his hat, calling out 'smile'. She walks faster, avoiding the drunken old man zig-zagging towards her, waving a polystyrene cup.

She follows her reflection in the shop windows along The Horsefair. She desperately needs to buy some new clothes, she thinks. On the corner of Merchant Street, she crosses to River Island, where Avril said she bought that dress in the shiny peach fabric. She wanders through the shop, scanning the rails of t-shirts, sweatshirts, jeans. She wants something glamorous, she thinks, picking up a silk blouse.

In the changing room, she slips the garment on, staring at her image in the mirrored cubicle wall. Beige suits her, she thinks. She could be at least seventeen, couldn't she? She'll ask Joe to come back with her later and see what he thinks. She checks her hair, pulls out the silver tube of lipstick from her bag and smoothes another layer of creamy lilac over her lips.

She weaves her way through Broadmead, past the hurrying, suited businessmen, the young woman wrapped in a grubby pink blanket outside Marks and Spencer's. At the top of Union Street, she stops by the entrance to Fairfax Precinct.

'Sam!' Joe is waving from across the street. He's wearing the red baseball jacket with white sleeves that she helped him choose from one of the vintage stalls in the flea market.

She crosses the road, and they kiss.

'We could get something to eat and go over to the docks,' he suggests, heading for his usual sandwich kiosk.

She walks with her hands shoved awkwardly into her jeans pockets. The scent of incense wafts along the dockside from the stalls selling ethnic jewellery, tie-dye t-shirts and garish scarves. Further along the cobbled street, families are sitting outside on the picnic benches by the burger van.

'You look really nice.' Joe screws up the greasy paper bag with the remains of his pie, tosses it into a litter bin. 'Kurt said I'm lucky to have such a pretty girlfriend.'

At the end of the quay, he leans against the iron railing. Across on the other side of the dock, white sailing boats are moored; the street is lined with trees and chic new bars.

'Can I have a cigarette?' she asks.

'I haven't got any.' He lifts his hands in the air, grinning. 'That's the surprise I wanted to tell you: I've stopped smoking! Kurt was great. We prayed together and asked God to take away the addiction right away. I've not wanted a cigarette since.'

'That's... good.'

He removes a Mars bar from the pocket where he usually tucks his cigarette packet and lighter, and unpeels the wrapper. 'I know what - why don't we get a film from the video shop and go back to mine? My dad won't mind giving you a lift home later.'

'All right.'

His face is solemn. 'I wanted to tell you, what happened to you last weekend was really amazing.' He takes her hand. 'It makes me so happy to see you letting God in. Now he can use us together to do amazing things.' He adjusts his baseball cap so that the peak faces backwards and gazes dreamily out across the harbour.

'I was wondering where you'd got to!' She keeps her eyes fixed on the T.V screen on the desk beside Joe's bed.

He moves to sit cross-legged next to her on top of the duvet. 'There you go.' He holds out a can of Diet Coke. 'One of my sister's. She's got a whole crate of the stuff.'

She makes no move to take it from him. 'Where've you been?'

'You know I had to phone Kurt: I told you. He had a few things he wanted to talk about.'

'You've been on the phone all this time?'

'They're still waiting for their new settees to arrive. The only things they have to sit on are Joyce and Graham Weaver's old kitchen chairs.'

'You've been talking about that, for an hour?'

'Not just that.' He lowers his voice. 'He wanted to ask my advice about Francesca. She's a bit down at the moment. Don't tell anyone, will you?'

'Of course I won't.'

'She doesn't want people to know. She hasn't made any friends yet and she thinks Portishead's depressing. I told him Bristol's got plenty of great places.'

'Is she okay? Francesca.'

'Kurt's going to take her out for a meal, to cheer her up. He asked if I knew anywhere nice.'

'He asked *you*?' She laughs.

'I told him to go to The Glass Boat: that restaurant on a boat by the docks.'

'I know where it is. You've never been there!'

'It's really romantic.'

'Just like you!' She shoves him. 'We're missing the film. D'you want to rewind it?'

'Na.' He shakes his head and pings open the ring pull on the can of Diet Coke.

'You've missed nearly all of it! It was you who wanted to watch Footloose.'

'How about this?' Joe had demanded in the video shop, waving the box for Ghostbusters in front of her.

She'd glanced at the cover. 'Mm... What about Lace 2? Or this one? Electric Dreams. Read the back - it looks really good.'

'No way!'

'Okay - The Blue Lagoon? Or Mad Max 3? You said you wanted to see that.'

'But they're 18s, Sam.'

Joe looks older than sixteen and can easily take out 18-certificate films. They usually watch them when their parents are out — or, they used to, she thinks.

He takes a swig of Diet Coke. 'Urgh! I don't know how you can drink this stuff!' He takes her hand, looking thoughtful for a moment. 'I might take you there, actually.'

'Where?'

'The Glass Boat. On your birthday.'

'Really?'

'Just leave it to me, okay?'

She touches his leg and he moves his arm around her, drawing her closer.

Six

Gifts

'I'll just be a minute.' Greta disappears up the staircase, leaving Sam waiting by the wood burning stove in the hallway.

'Hi, Sam!' Greta's mother calls from the kitchen. 'Come on through.'

Lou is peering into the circular, stand-up mirror perched on the breakfast table, surrounded by tubes of foundation, compacts, eye-liner and lip-liner pencils, an assortment of various sized make-up brushes. Her red hair is scraped back from her face with a band. 'You might as well sit down. You know what Greta's like.'

'Thanks.' Sam pulls a stool out from under the table. 'Are you working tonight?'

'Just in Bristol.' Lou picks up the fattest brush, flicking beige powder onto her nose and cheeks. 'At the Thekla.'

'Really?' she replies. She's never heard of it.

She watches Lou's reflection in the mirror shade a blue line onto the lid of her closed eye, then take one of the finer brushes, gently smudging the colour across her eyelid.

Sunlight steams across the table through the bay window. Outside, red, pink and purple flowers hang in baskets from uneven white-washed walls. Tall white sails protrude from the boatyard behind the garage door, upon which Lou has painted a fat yellow sun.

Lou swiftly smoothes mascara onto her eyelashes and tugs the band from her head. Glossy red hair falls to frame her face, halting sharply at her shoulders. She looks so glamorous, Sam thinks, in her black dress, cut low at the waist; she could be a model.

'Where are you two off to tonight?'

'Er, the youth meeting.'

'That's right.' She scoops up the make-up, transferring it to a pile on the sideboard, along with the ashtrays, rusty keys, pens, pencils, screw-drivers, nail files, rizla papers. 'Greta said the new leaders are a bit whacky, hey?' She smiles at Sam; her eyes are quite startling now, circled in grey kohl.

Greta flounces into the kitchen. 'Let's go! Bye, Mum.' She kisses Lou on the cheek

'See you later, darling. I'll be back about twelve-thirty. Make sure you're in bed by ten, okay?'

'I think this is it.' Sam examines the crumpled sheet of paper. On Sunday, they were all given a photocopy of the hand-sketched map, but the directions are from the M5 to Kurt's house, not for anyone arriving via the housing estates, on the Badgerline bus from Clevedon.

'God, I'd hate to live in one of these!' Greta eyes the rows of lego-like houses. They're in the middle of a new estate; dusty machinery is parked at the end of the street where houses are still half-built. 'Wouldn't you?'

'They're all right.'

'There's no soul!'

'Don't be an idiot!'

Greta stubs out her cigarette on the ground with her sandal. 'Are you *sure* Joe's given up smoking?'

'That's what he said.'

'Well, good for him, as long as we don't all have to copy him.'

The silhouette of Francesca in a green dress appears behind the frosted glass doorway. 'Hi girls! Come on in! It's just through here.'

The small, square living room is already full; members of the youth group are squeezed in two lines along the pink floral settees. Upright chairs and cushions have been placed around the edges of room for additional people.

Joe occupies one of the pine chairs, his guitar poised on his knee. He is engrossed in conversation with Kurt and hasn't noticed her come in. She places herself beside Greta on the navy carpet by the window.

Francesca drags over a chair beside them. Her bottle-green dress is sleeveless, emphasising her toned arms. 'Isn't this weather glorious? Is it always this warm here in May?'

Greta shakes her head. 'This is unusual. It's a shame we have to be indoors.'

'I agree,' Francesca smiles. 'We'll have a picnic in the park one evening, shall we? Before the summer ends.'

'Let's make a start.' Kurt beams around the room. 'First of all, thanks to Joe.' He pats Joe on the shoulder, warmly. 'Our friend here has agreed to be our praise and worship leader. And he's gonna start us off this evening.'

Joe strums the introduction to 'Shine your love.' They rise to their feet, singing along with him, '*Jesus, shine the light of your love in the darkness… Shine your love, fill this world with your splendour; blaze, like a fire, in our hearts.*'

The transformation in Joe is astonishing: he's so full of light, so full of God. She forces her gaze away, glancing at Francesca beside her: her eyes are closed. Some of the group have their hands raised; Kurt is absorbed in his own private worship dance in the corner by the television.

Joe leads them into a slower song, '*Be silent for the Spirit is moving here…*'

Aware of her close proximity to Francesca, she murmurs the words. She's never liked singing. In their old church, her father used to ask Stella and herself to stand at the front sometimes and sing a chorus for the congregation; the older members liked it. Stella had enjoyed all the attention, but not her. She has to sing now, she thinks, or look stupid. Not that Greta cares: she's not even pretending to try.

The song tails off and Joe continues to play the tune softly. Around the room, some of the group pray aloud and speak in tongues.

The room gradually falls silent. Around the circle, eyes are shut; Joe's hands are raised; Greta is sitting cross-legged, in the cotton flares she's dyed purple, her face hidden by a mass of thick, blonde hair.

'God wants to tell you he is grieving,' Kurt says, his tone serious. 'Your hearts are closed to him. You must realise the urgency of the task he has given you. God has given *all* of you his gifts of the Spirit: tongues, a holy language to praise him; prophesy and interpretation, for him to speak to us directly; his healing power. God is saying to you today, if you don't use his gifts, you *cannot* carry out his work.'

The room is silent once more; there's a chill coming from the open window. She retreats behind the safety of her closed eyelids. 'God, please fill me with the Holy Spirit again,' she prays, in her head, 'so that I can use your gifts.'

She waits. The daylight outside has turned to dusk. Cold air brushes against her skin as the Spirit moves around the room; she jams her hands between her knees to keep them still.

Kurt speaks again. 'God is saying there is someone here tonight who's rebelling against him. He wants you to know he understands how hard it is for you right now, how hard it is to change. God wants you to know that your family in Christ loves you. We are praying for you, we are waiting for you and we will keep on praying. Nothing is too difficult for him.'

She keeps her eyes shut tightly.

Kurt whispers something to Joe, who picks up his guitar, strumming the chords to 'O Lord, how we have fallen!'

The group sing quietly, '...*the fires of darkness burn. You grieve to see your commands of love so shattered, and lives in ruins. O Lord, how we have fallen!*'

They have reached Greta's street and she still isn't speaking; she's been quiet all the way back on the bus. Her face is pale, her expression strange.

'Are you okay?' Sam asks.

'Yep.' She isn't even going to ask her into the house.

'You sure you're all right?'

'I said yes.' Greta darts up the path to the sky blue front door, fumbles with the key, and vanishes inside.

Seven

Chosen

Jack O'Conner, from the second year, has installed himself in their tutor room, his creased white shirt hanging over faded ripped jeans with buckled leather boots. They can't escape because they have to stay here for the whole of morning break, manning the chocolate fudge cake stall. Jack slipped a note into Greta's locker on Wednesday morning, declaring his feelings for her and asking her out. Sam was sent to find him during lunch-break. 'She says you're really sweet, but way too young for her.'

It's made no difference: every time Sam glances in Jack's direction, he's grinning, stupidly, at her friend.

Each tutor group has come up with ideas to raise money for Charities Week, the classroom desks transformed into stalls running raffles and competitions. Their three trays of chocolate fudge cake, created on Monday night in an attempt to avoid ominous growing piles of revision, have almost sold out. It'll be a relief when the last slice is gone, she thinks, having consumed too much sickly fudge topping.

Mr Allen appears in their tutor room, eating a fairy cake. 'Hello, girls.'

Greta dishes him a wide smile. 'Would you like to buy some chocolate cake, Sir?' It's Mufti day, and Greta is adorned in a pair of shorts that she constructed herself, unpicking the stitches down the middle of her navy shorts and khaki shorts, and sewing the odd halves together. She's wearing black laddered tights, has painted her nails dark green and backcombed her usually silky, blonde hair.

Mr Allen winks. 'I'd better not: this is my fourth cake. I just came to give these back.' He holds out the practice exam essays Sam handed in last week. She'd missed his last English lesson due to an interview with the Careers Advisor.

'Thanks.' She gazes fondly at the greasy finger marks he's left on the front page beside the circled A.

'I thought it might spur you on with the revision. Greta, I still haven't had all of yours.'

'I have *done* them!' Greta states. 'I left them at home.'

'Well, bring them in on Monday then!'

'I'd better do some work this weekend,' her friend groans, when he's gone. 'I've not even started!'

'You can't tomorrow.'

'Why not?' Greta rubs her head. 'Oh God, I forgot! London!'

They saunter along Marine Hill. The swaying trees are heavy with rain. Greta, who won't use an umbrella, runs her fingers through her saturated hair; water drips from the end of her fringe, her nose, her lips. 'I keep meaning to tell you, I saw Francesca the other night.'

'Really? Where?'

'Out running along the promenade. I think it was her. It was dark and pissing it down; she must have got soaked.'

'Was Kurt with her?'

Greta shakes her head. 'No, just her.'

Sam holds her hand outside the sheltered perimeter of her red umbrella; it's still raining hard. 'What d'you think of Kurt?'

'A bit short and stocky. I prefer tall men with long legs and-'

'Not like that! As a person.'

'He's a jerk!'

'Greta!'

'*You* asked me!'

'Joe's so pally with him: it's getting on my nerves.'

'Is he *still*?'

'He talks to him practically every day. More than me.'

'That's weird!' It's warm out, despite the downpour, and Greta peels off her wet jacket, slinging it over her school bag. 'Bloody typical Joe.'

'He says Kurt's really spiritual: he's always going off for days on his own to speak to God.'

Greta laughs. 'And we're supposed to be impressed?'

They have reached the corner where Sam turns left into Holly Lane and Greta continues along Marine Hill towards the promenade.

'It's meant to be nice tomorrow. What're you wearing?'

Greta shrugs. 'Hey, d'you think we'll be able to go off on our own in London?'

Most of the congregation have come on the trip to the Royal Albert Hall: some on the coach; the rest having made their own way, meeting up with the coach party at two o'clock for the picnic in Kensington

Gardens.

'So, Sam, what do you want to do when you're older?' Kurt asks her.

Kurt and Francesca have been donated her parents' tartan picnic blanket, leaving Sam, Joe and Greta sitting cross-legged on the grass. Her mother and father are perched on fold-up chairs, her mum dishing out rolls filled with layers of bright orange cheese and her dad pouring tea and orangeade into plastic cups.

'I er... I don't know yet.'

'What about you, Greta?' Kurt bites into a baguette, bursting with ham.

'I might become a firewoman,' Greta replies, nonchalantly. 'It must be amazing to do something worthwhile like that.'

Joe hoots with laughter. 'Yeah, right! The training nearly kills you. You have to lift heavy men down ladders.' He has turned up the collar of his baseball jacket, just like the collar of Kurt's leather jacket.

'I'd like a word with these girls, if you don't mind,' Francesca interrupts, casting Joe an irritated glance and moving to sit on the grass beside Sam and Greta.

They swivel to face her, away from the others. She looks exotic, Sam thinks, in her denim jacket and jeans, her glossy hair tumbling over her shoulders; her hair is layered, she notices.

'There's a few things Kurt and I want to get going over the next few weeks; Kurt will explain all of it in the youth meeting. I'm hoping to set up some meetings in schools. Would you two help me?'

The windows switch from the stark light of the platform to black as the tube whirs and jolts into the tunnel. Greta unclasps her rucksack and produces two cans of Pils lager.

'Where did you get those from?'

'One of Mum's boyfriends left them - Danny, from Cardiff. Oh yeah, I didn't tell you...' Greta pings back the ring-pull and takes a swig of beer from the can. 'You know Scott? Sarah's boyfriend.'

'Sarah from the youth group?'

Greta nods.

'I didn't know she had a boyfriend.'

'That's cos he's never been to church or anything, and he's older - he left school two years ago.'

'How do *you* know?'

'He's always in The Wagon and Horses, where Grandad goes. I've only spoken to him a couple of times. Anyway, he called round on Wednesday night; he said he hoped I didn't mind him just turning up but he was upset - Sarah'd just told him she didn't want to go out with him anymore.'

'Really? D'you think he likes you?'

'Oh God, no! He's mad on Sarah. He thought I might be able to talk to her or something. He keeps trying to change himself to get her to like him more: not drinking, quitting smoking, taking his earring out. I told him that was really dumb.'

'Totally!'

'I'd never change myself just for someone else. Would *you*? I mean, how would you know whether someone really likes you or not, if they want you to be something you're not?'

They remain on the tube until it has stopped at every station on the Circle Line, disembarking again at South Kensington station. They run the two streets to the Royal Albert Hall. An usher directs them up a narrow staircase at the side of the entrance lobby.

'Welcome to another National Christian Fellowship Celebration.' The speaker's voice rings warmly across the hall. 'Do you know how many Christians there are here tonight? Ten thousand! Let's give our thanks to God together for that!'

The roar of clapping and cheering resounds through the building. It's too late to find the rest of their party; Joe isn't anywhere in sight. They've ended up sitting high in the gallery; far below, she can see the tiny figure of her father on the stage with the other ministers, and Joe's father, seated by the drums with the musicians.

'My second point is that we need to *fear* God.'

The speaker seems to have been talking for hours, or perhaps the can of lager has made her sleepy.

'If we feared God, we wouldn't treat our relationship with him so casually. We would continually be in awe of who he is and our relationship with him would become very precious.'

Greta nudges her and mimes the action of inhaling on a cigarette. They'll need to slip out of the building in time for her to find somewhere to smoke before they join the coach.

'We would be humble before him. We would fall flat on our faces before him during worship times. We must be servants, willing and ready to serve him in any way...'

'Come on!' Greta whispers, clutching her rucksack.

'Hang on! Just wait a minute!'

They have a birds-eye view of the events on the stage: the miniscule people, like toy figures, coming up onto the platform to be prayed for by the leaders; those springing out of wheelchairs, walking triumphantly up and down the aisles; the two blind people raising their hands to heaven because God has restored their sight; the deaf man, crying in amazement into the microphone, 'I can hear! Thank the Lord! I can hear again!'

Eight

Meetings

'Coming round later?' Greta is wearing one of her father's old white shirts, hitched in at the waist with a black PVC belt but it still looks ten sizes too large.

'Who cares?' she'd said, when Suzanne Matthews commented, 'Nice school uniform!' earlier in double Maths.

None of the teachers, with the exception of Mrs Twist, is bothered about whether or not their uniform is correct anymore. The familiar tickings-off have been replaced with warnings: serious words, like 'the future' and 'the rest of your lives', as though they might have forgotten that their exams are beginning imminently or how much revision they still must complete.

'Okay, I'll bring my bike.'

'D'you want to get chips again?'

The last two Friday nights, they've cycled along the seafront to the beach café behind Body Bliss Fitness and bought plates of chips with tomato ketchup.

'Fermez vos cahiers, s'il vous plait.' Miss May waits by the blackboard, her chin tilted back, surveying the classroom.

Noticing the teacher's disapproving glance, Sam stops talking and looks towards the blackboard.

Miss May offers her nod of approval. 'Alors! L'examinations commencerent dans un mois.'

In the past, the French teacher has used this moment, when she has their attention at the end of the lesson, to complain: 'G2 is the worst class in the school.' Instead, she now adds to the increasing pressure being placed on all of them to spend their whole lives revising: 'Si vous voulez les passer, c'est imperative que vous faites un grand effort maintenant. D'accord?'

She stands purposefully, her back held straight, her pastel yellow blouse and skirt emphasizing the curves of her breasts and hips. 'Cary, Julia, Matthew et Sam, restez ici apres le lesson, s'il vous plait. Levez vous la class.'

Metal chair legs squeak and scrape on the floor.

'Au revoir, la class.'

'Au revoir, Mademoiselle May.'

'Assayez vous...'

Sam takes a seat in the row directly in front of Miss May's desk, beside Julia Lamb and Cary Bell. She glances anxiously towards the glass panelled door: Julia's and Cary's names have cropped up in school jokes since the first year, for working studiously and being awarded copious Commendation Certificates in school assemblies.

'Bon... I've asked you four to stay behind because you are my best pupils. You are all capable of achieving high A grades in your GCSE's.' She gazes at each of them intently. 'Can you get out your exercise books?'

Sam retrieves the blue French book from her school bag. They were asked to decorate them in the first week of the year; hers is covered with pictures of French café scenes cut out of a glossy Thompson's brochure for romantic weekends in Paris.

'Open your books at the back and turn them upside down - that's right. Now put today's date.'

They scribble obediently.

'Good. Now, I'm going to set you some advanced work. The exercises on these worksheets are a higher level than the work we're doing in class - I would give these to A level students - but I'm sure you won't find them too difficult.' She hands each of them a wad of papers. 'Complete them by next week, please, and keep this work in the back of your books.'

The teacher's handwriting is the same on the sheets as on the blackboard: small spidery letters with wide spaces between each word.

'I'd like us to meet in my classroom every Tuesday lunchtime until the exam. I'm prepared to give up my lunch hour to teach you.' Miss May smiles. 'There's no need to mention this to anyone else.'

Greta is waiting for her in their tutor room. 'You've been ages!'

She lifts her sleeve to glance at her watch: they're five minutes late. Francesca will be waiting.

'And you left me with Jack O'Connor, hanging about to see I was going for lunch in the dinner hall. I didn't tell him about Christian Union in case he wanted to come.'

'Sorry. How did you get rid of him?'

'Don't ask! Why did Miss May want to see you?'

'We have to do extra work.'

'What?'

'Because, "You are my best pupils."' She lilts her voice and sticks out her chest. 'I'm prepared to give up my lunch break to teach you.'

Greta frowns. 'What, just you four?'

'We're not supposed to tell anybody.'

'That's not fair! My mum's been taking me to stay with Marie-Louise since I was five. I can already speak French!'

'At least you don't have extra work.'

In reception, Mr Harris is conversing with Francesca, beaming ridiculously, his face even redder than usual. 'Ah, yes! Your young helpers.' He waves in their direction, as though addressing his favourite pupils. 'If you'd like to come with me, ladies, I'll show you the room.'

They had accompanied Francesca to meet Mr Harris last week. It was the first time Sam had set foot in the headmaster's office; Greta had been summoned in before at various points over the years, when she'd accumulated one too many detentions.

He was surprisingly helpful when Francesca suggested organising the Christian Union group. 'Yes, yes, what a marvellous idea! You can use the conference room adjacent to my office.'

She and Greta were given permission to pin up posters on the notice boards in the school corridors and classrooms, and the headmaster said he'd make a special announcement himself in assembly.

'I might pop along and show my support,' he says now, positioning himself even closer to Francesca.

'You've been so kind,' Francesca smiles. 'I'm sure this will be a success.' She glances towards the group of first years hovering shyly by reception. 'It looks like our first arrivals are here!'

Mr Harris retreats hastily behind the closed door of his office.

The Christian Union is popular with the lower school: boys with glasses and spots; chubby girls with frizzy hair who still wear knee-high white bobble socks. Some of the girls from the church youth group - Maria Davies, Sarah McIvor - have come along to show their support. Everyone is seated around the long conference table, munching on their packed lunches.

Francesca moves between the different groups; 'Call me Francesca.' The soft fabric of her blouse and light skirt stands out amidst the A-line skirts, stiff-collared shirts and school ties that the rest of them are assigned.

Sam, sitting with Greta at the far end of the table, opens the Tupperware lunchbox - containing the cheese sandwiches and Wagon Wheel - that her mother packed for her. Greta unwraps cling film from two dubious looking peanut butter sandwiches that have been squashed in the bottom of her bag.

'School dinner's fish fingers and chips today,' she frowns. 'And chocolate sponge.'

'Yeah, but you'd have had to sit next to Jack O'Conner.'

'That's true.' Greta rolls her eyes towards Julia Lamb. 'How come she's so skinny?'

Julia is sitting in front of them, slowly ploughing through rolls, cheese and onion crisps, slices of cake wrapped in tin foil, chocolate biscuits, snack-size boxes of nuts and raisins, a triple pack of Jaffa Orange Juice cartons.

'Let's start the meeting with a prayer, shall we?' Francesca announces, in her calm, clear voice. 'Lord Jesus, I thank you for bringing each of us here to share together today. I ask that you will use us to shine out and be a witness for you in this school. Amen.'

She opens her eyes to rest on Francesca, standing elegantly by the flip chart at the head of the table. It seems strange, being in school with *her*.

'As you know, we're going to meet every Friday lunchtime. I'd like some of *your* ideas. What would *you* like from these meetings? Could you get into groups of three or four for a few minutes and jot down some of your thoughts? Then we'll hear everyone's ideas at the end and I'll take them away and come up with a programme for next week. Come and collect some paper from the front.'

Julia Lamb and Maria Davies drag over their chairs to join Sam and Greta.

'I'd like Bible studies and prayer meetings,' Julia says, unpeeling the silver and green wrapper from another mint chocolate Yoyo.

Maria scribbles 'Bible studies' and 'Prayer meetings' on the sheet of flip chart paper with a fat marker pen. 'What about singing?'

Francesca approaches their group. 'How're we doing?'

Sam frantically tries to think of a good idea.

'Would it be possible to meet up with Christian Unions in other schools?' Maria asks, evidently trying to make an impression.

'What a brilliant idea! I'll certainly look into it.'

'How about trips?' Greta says. 'To Alton Towers… or horse riding?'

'That'd be nice.' Francesca smiles, encouragingly, from Greta to Sam. 'Would you two be able to help me put together a schedule for the term?'

How wonderful it is, Sam thinks, to be getting to know her.

Nine

Resistance

'Guess what!' Greta smirks.

Sam grips onto the metal rail as the bus swings past The Broadway Hotel into South Road. 'What?'

'Shannon Gardner's going out with Leanne Jackson.'

Most of the girls in the school fancy Shannon, who looks ten years older than all the other boys. Everyone knows he lost his virginity when he was twelve years old, to an older woman.

'I thought he was seeing Carlotta Woods.'

'Apparently, he got off with Leanne in Spirals, in front of Carlotta's mates and everyone.'

'Really?'

'It's true! Connor Cartwright told me, today in Geography.'

'D'you still like him?'

Greta went out with Shannon for a couple of weeks last summer, until it became clear that he only wanted to have sex with her. It was probably for the best that she packed him in because, since then, he's gone through half the girls in their year.

Greta pulls a face. 'You must be joking!'

'Come out the back and I'll show you my new purchase.' Francesca leads them through the kitchen into the garden. 'I found them in B&Q this afternoon. Aren't they neat?'

Sam and Greta smile politely at the cerise plastic table and chairs.

'Take a seat and I'll fetch us something to drink. I've made pink lemonade.'

'Great.'

'I love those.' Francesca points to Greta's trousers.

'Thanks. I tie-dyed them.'

'You'll have to tell me how you did it.'

Francesca disappears into the kitchen, returning with a jug of lemonade, three glasses and a notebook tucked under her arm. 'You see! This is perfect for entertaining, and getting a tan.'

Sam squints in the sun. 'You're already tanned.'

'Oh, it's faded. I've not been on a sunbed since we left California.'

'Do you belong to a gym?' Greta asks.

'I did. I've not got round to joining anywhere here yet.'

'My mum goes to Body Bliss Fitness in Clevedon, at the end of the promenade. There's a pool and bar and stuff.'

'I'll have to check it out.' Cubes of ice clunk against the inside of the jug as Francesca pours the lemonade. 'Thanks for all your help last Friday. It went well, didn't it?'

'Yeah, it was good.' Sam picks up her glass of pink liquid. 'There were loads of first years, though. It'd be better if more fifth years came, and sixth formers.'

'That's certainly something to think about: bringing in a wider range of ages.'

'And more boys,' Greta adds.

Francesca nods. 'There weren't many boys. I was thinking, a different name might attract more people. What do you think? Christian Union sounds a bit old-fashioned, doesn't it?'

'What about Allsorts? As in, all sorts of people go to church,' Greta suggests. 'Or Jigsaw? Like, you know, we're all pieces of a puzzle.'

'I like that! Jigsaw it is, then. Now, shall I show you what I've done?' She flips open the notebook and hands them each a sheet of paper. 'Those are just draft copies of the programme. See what you think. I can change anything if you have any better ideas.'

She scans the list: Francesca has allocated a different topic and speaker to each Friday. Her father's name is down, she notices, to speak about witnessing to friends; Kurt is talking about 'Our relationship with God'; Robin, from the youth group, is pencilled in with a question mark to lead 'From Drugs to Christ'. Robin gave his harrowing testimony in church last month about how the Lord saved him from his addiction.

'If you see there,' Francesca points to the bottom of the sheet, 'I've put a note about after school prayer meetings on Tuesdays.'

Greta doesn't look enthralled. 'What about trips?'

'I wanted to talk to you about that, Greta. I was wondering if you'd be the social secretary? Be in charge of arranging outings?'

Her face lightens. 'Yeah, I can do that.'

'I know you had a few good ideas on Friday, but don't forget we're going to Alton Towers with the youth group in August and Ben's trying to organise for everyone to go pony trekking, so some different activities would-'

'We could go to the beach for the day. Porthcawl's not far: there's a brilliant fair.'

'And perhaps a swimming trip would be easy to organise,' Francesca adds, 'or a barbeque? Could you have a think about it, and perhaps you could say something to everyone on Friday?'

'Okay.'

'And Sam, I was hoping you might be in charge of putting together a newsletter, say, once a term? Think you could manage that?'

There are voices sounding from the kitchen: the others arriving for the youth meeting.

Francesca reaches across the table and pats her hand. 'I'll talk to you more about it next time. Thanks, you guys. I couldn't do this without you.'

She knew this was going to happen, as soon as she heard the announcement on Sunday about the event being organised for the visiting American youth group.

Joe puts his arm around her. 'I'll see you at the church party tomorrow; everyone's invited to that. I can stay 'til eight.'

'But tomorrow's my birthday!'

'And these are Kurt's guests, all the way from California, and he's asked some of us, especially, to be hosts.'

'But you said about us going to The Glass Boat.'

He draws his arm away abruptly. 'You're so selfish! Where's your sense of what's important?'

'What?'

'I'm talking about your commitment to God, if you hadn't realised!' He swings around and strides briskly towards the kitchen, leaving her standing alone in the garden.

She trails behind him into the house.

Greta has saved her a place on the navy carpet. 'What's the matter with Joe?'

She shrugs. Joe has found a chair on the other side of the room; he's refusing to look at her. She's never seen him like this before.

Kurt frowns in the direction of Ben and Avril, who've just started going out together and are joking around about who should sit on the last floor cushion; they've agreed to share it but Avril keeps slipping off the side.

Once Kurt has everyone's undivided attention, he begins, 'This morning, when I woke up, God told me he had something very important to say to me and I needed to go someplace quiet. So I drove along the coast, to a little place called Breen Sands. I sat on the beach - there was no-one around - and God spoke to me. He reminded me how important our work is and he told me we need to think bigger; God wants us to expand our outreach, first in the city, then the whole country. The possibilities are endless!'

He moves his gaze slowly around the room from person to person. 'As I've already told some of you, we've established a Youth Ministry Team: Joe, Robin, Pippa, Nick, Francesca and myself. This team will meet regularly to pray and seek God's direction, not just for our group but the whole church. I want these individuals to join me at the front at the end of the Sunday services, to pray for those who come forward. God wants to see them healing the sick, leading the way for the church!'

Joe makes eye contact with her for a moment across the room, then looks away, his lips pressed tightly together.

'The next thing is outreach.' Kurt's blue eyes are bright and animated. 'How can we reach the young people across the city who don't go to church, who don't hear the message?' He pauses for them all to consider this. 'God is beginning to give me a picture, a vision of a meeting where thousands of young people are brought together and touched by God's power. This is what we're looking to in the future. I want you all to pray for God's guidance in the coming weeks as we move towards making this a reality.'

'Okay,' Kurt gives Joe a hearty pat on the back, 'let's praise God for all the exciting things he's doing in our lives.'

Joe picks up his guitar and begins playing: '*Give us more devotion (give us more devotion), give us more power (give us more power)...*' The boys sing each of the lines first, the girls repeating them. '*And I will praise you with all of my love, and I will praise you with all of my will, and I will praise you with all of my strength, for you are my God...*'

Joe slows the song into open worship; around the room, one or two members of the group pray aloud, foreign words flowing from their mouths. 'Dear God,' she asks, silently, 'please help me to speak in tongues now.'

The room falls quiet as Kurt waits for each of them to let the Spirit in. Some are standing with their eyes closed and hands raised;

others shuffle awkwardly and sit down. She is growing hotter, her skin damp and clammy.

At last, Kurt speaks: 'God is saying, why do you continue to close your hearts to him? He needs you to become an empty container so he can fill you with his Spirit. Instead, you're full of your own problems.'

Across the room, Joe is gazing at Kurt, his face full of concern. The group grows still again while they wait for something further to happen. She can feel the Spirit hover like a thunder cloud, pressing against her chest. She's been filled with the Holy Spirit, hasn't she? Or is she a fraud? If she's genuinely filled with the Spirit, why can't she speak in tongues?

'God is saying to you,' Joe reads sombrely from the Bible propped open on his lap, 'For you are still unspiritual, under the control of ordinary impulses... of the flesh, behaving yourselves after a human standard and like mere unchanged men.'

This heaviness, she knows, is her resistance: she's blocking God. She glances at Francesca: her soft silhouette in the darkening room, her lowered eyelids. If only Francesca could help her.

'I need to talk to you,' Joe murmurs, under his breath, in the hallway.

'What about?'

'Not here.'

'Okay. But can't you tell me what it's about?'

'No.' He glances around, edgily. 'It'll have to be tomorrow, before the party.'

Ten

Commitment

She crosses Prince Street onto the quayside. Joe is leaning against one of the iron benches outside the Watershed. He has on the smoky-grey t-shirt she bought him for his sixteenth birthday, tucked into grey jeans. His blond hair has a glossy sheen in the sunlight, which is still surprisingly strong for the early evening.

He kisses her - 'Happy birthday!' - stooping to pick up the flat cardboard box propped against the seat.

'Thanks,' she smiles.

They sit side by side on the bench, Sam balancing the box between her knees. She unpeels the Sellotape, prizing open the cardboard lid and tugging out an enormous padded card made of shiny red fabric. On the front is a picture of a teddy bear clutching a bunch of red roses. Beneath the rhyme inside, Joe has scrawled his name in sloping letters, with a neat row of kisses.

He turns to unclip his rucksack, producing a small rectangular package. 'This is for you, too.'

She takes the gift and carefully removes the pink and gold striped paper, revealing a cassette tape. 'The Eurythmics! Thanks!'

'I couldn't decide between that or Chris de Burgh.'

'I prefer this.' She leans across to kiss him on the cheek. 'I wish we could do something together later.'

A look of annoyance flickers across his face. 'I thought I'd explained, I have to go to this meal. Kurt's asked everyone in the Ministry Team to meet his friends; they've come all the way from America.'

She stares down at the picture of Annie Lennox through the see-through plastic cassette case.

'You'd be coming too if... Well, that's what I wanted to talk to you about.'

'What?'

'When I went round to Kurt and Francesca's the other night to talk about the Youth Ministry Team, you should have been there with me.'

'But I wasn't-'

'Do you know why you weren't?' He watches her intently.

'I hadn't really thought.' She runs her fingers over the crumpled wrapping paper, smoothing out the creases.

'You have to put your life right, Sam.'

'What's wrong with my life?'

'You know what I mean. You need to take your relationship with God more seriously.'

'But I *am* serious.' She breaks away from his gaze, fixing her eyes on one of the white sailing boats moored to the dockside.

'Haven't you listened to what Kurt's said in the meetings?'

'But I have.'

'How often do you pray?

'I do sometimes.'

'You see! You should talk to God all the time, like a friend. And read the Bible.'

'I *am* going to read the Bible more, after my exams have finished.'

'Exactly! You're putting a few silly exams before God. You're not living a hundred percent for him.'

'They're not, I mean, I am-'

'You have to open your mind to what he wants to say to you so he can use you to speak to others. Like when God told me I needed to talk to you today.'

'You're right. I will, okay?' She folds the wrapping paper and slips it with the cassette into her bag. 'We'd better go to the party.'

'There's no hurry. Kurt knows I'm talking to you.'

She swings around. 'You've told him?'

'Kurt and I talk about everything. It was him who was most concerned about Greta.'

'Greta? What's she got to do with it?'

'I need to talk to you about her; it's important.'

'Why don't you talk to her yourself?'

'There's no need to defend her. I understand how hard it is for you.'

'Nothing's hard for me.'

'You know... Her being the way she is, and she's your friend and everything.'

'She's my best friend!'

'You know what I'm talking about.' He's deep in thought, his eyes fixed on the bench between them; the green paint is flaking from the metal rungs. 'I'm praying for her; Kurt's spoken to me and he's praying for her; Francesca, everyone in the youth group: they're all praying for her.'

'Francesca never said anything.'

'Everyone knows she's got problems with God: smoking and drinking and whatever else she does. She doesn't want to change. But the thing that worries me most is she's holding you back.'

She looks away. A group of women in short dresses and skirts, heels emphasising long pale legs, clatter across Prince Street Bridge; their laughter echoes along the street.

'It's the Devil who's making her difficult, making her hardened. You can help her, but you need to help yourself first.'

She rubs her face with her hands; her mind is fuzzy.

'I think you should speak to Kurt and Francesca about it,' he states, firmly.

'No!'

'They care, so let them help.'

It is seven-thirty when they arrive at the museum; the party is almost over. Not that it's much of a party, anyway. Her mother and Evelyn Winstanley are serving tea, coffee and jugs of orange squash through the hatch between the kitchen and the main hall. The chairs have been cleared to the edges of the room so that people can mingle. A trestle table has been set up at one end, with plates of sausage rolls, squares of cheese and pickled onions on sticks, slices of Quiche Lorraine; bowls of lettuce and tomatoes, peanuts, crisps; Tupperware containers of iced sponge cakes provided by Joyce Weaver.

On Sunday, her father asked as many members of the congregation as possible to come along to greet the American visitors, but hardly any of the youth group has turned up. Robin and Nick are talking over by the platform, dressed in suits. Pippa is hovering close to Kurt and a tall, young man who looks like he could be a model for a car advert, giggling at some joke passed between them. She's all dressed up, Sam notices, in that low-cut dress, crimson lipstick, her peroxide blonde hair flicked and fixed in perfect place. Francesca is conversing with another group of Americans; she's wearing a deep blue dress, closely-fitted, the sleeves ruffled and cut to a v-shape over the backs of her hands. They're all heading off to The Hole in the Wall in ten minutes.

She hovers awkwardly beside Joe. After their conversation earlier, everything else seems too trivial to be worth talking about. At least Greta's not here, she thinks; it's bad enough, having to face Kurt and Francesca. What have they said about her?

At quarter to eight, the room empties as the group of Americans exit. Jo squeezes her hand and makes his departure with them. Her father asks some of the men to help manoeuvre the chairs back into rows for a time of prayer and thanksgiving before the rest of them undertake their journeys home. There is no-one left below the age of thirty.

'Come and sit beside me, dear.' Margery Henderson, who attends the women's prayer group with her mother, links her arm through Sam's, patting her hand warmly, reminding her of when she was a child: all the ladies in their Sunday hats used to make a fuss of Stella and herself.

Members of the congregation stand, one by one. 'Thank you, Lord, for this time that we've been able to share together tonight.'

'Lord, we give you praise for this wonderful building that you've provided for us.'

'Lord, we thank you for healing Burt Partridge's sister of cancer.'

'We give you thanks, Lord, for the birth of Malcolm and Alison's new baby boy.'

The room falls quiet. The meeting is winding to a close, thank goodness; she's desperate to go home.

But not quite: Veronica Neal is on her feet, beginning another prayer. Veronica is tall and skinny, with masses of blonde wiry curls falling to her waist. Every week in church she dances at the back of the service, flinging her arms around, and her knitting needles click throughout the sermons. 'Thank you, Lord,' she says, dolefully, 'for curing my acne at last.'

'Did you have a nice time with Joe?' Her mother is sitting beside her in the back seat of the car. Jean Hutton has been given the front passenger seat on account of her bad hips; they're dropping her off in Nailsea on the way home.

'It was all right.'

'What did you do?'

'Nothing really.' The box containing the padded birthday card is pressed between her legs and the passenger door. She picks at the torn

Sellotape hanging from the lid.

'Didn't you want to go out for the meal with them all?'

'Not really.' She stares glumly through the car window. The motorway is unusually quiet: at nine o'clock on a Friday night, everyone is already somewhere they want to be.

'I suppose there were a lot of people going. What a shame Greta didn't come with you tonight.'

She shrugs.

'I'm sorry it's not been much of a birthday for you, love. Why don't you plan something special for tomorrow?'

'I dunno. I'll ring Greta.'

'We could call in to see her on the way past. Would that cheer you up?'

'Could we? I know she'll be at home; her mum's out working.'

'Why don't you ask her to come back to our house? I'll treat you to a pizza.'

She smiles. 'Thanks, Mum.'

Eleven

Demons

Sam rests the plastic tray, holding two empty glasses and a packet of salt and vinegar crisps, on the pink carpet. She sits, cross-legged, on the spongy sleeping bag opposite Greta. 'Why did you want glasses?'

'Hold on.' Greta scrambles for something inside her rucksack. 'Here you go!' She produces a small dusty bottle and several tatty paperbacks. 'Happy birthday, again!'

'What's that?'

'Brandy, from the back of the medicine cabinet. It's been there years.'

'And these?' She picks up one of the books, The Island Prince.

'Mum's read them. They're Mills and Boon - all about sex.'

She gazes at the faded image of a man standing beneath a palm tree, his white shirt swept open, revealing his tanned muscular chest.

'Hey, the trousers look good on you!' Greta smiles at the present she gave her in tutor period this morning.

Sam turns to look in the dressing table mirror. 'I love the material.' The fabric is patterned with deep purple and green swirls. Joe didn't even notice them.

'From one of Mum's old hippy dresses. She said the colours'd suit you.'

'You should be a designer when you're older. You could have your own shop.'

'Mm.' Greta tears open the packet of crisps, tipping the contents onto the tray. 'What about you then?'

'I don't know.'

'You must have some idea. If you could do anything?'

'...I'd become a lawyer, get married, have two children, and travel round the world.'

'You won't be able to travel with children.'

'I might! That's what your mum did. Are you sure she won't mind you staying over?'

'She won't notice. I'll be home before she's awake.'

'Don't you get scared sleeping in the house on your own?'

'I can always go to Gran's, can't I?' Greta points to the brandy bottle; 'Are you going to open it?'

She fills the tumblers, shaking the last drops of liquor from the bottle and pushing the glasses together to check they contain an equal amount.

'After three!' Greta takes one of the drinks, holding it poised beside her mouth. 'Ready?'

She waves her hand, laughing.

'One… two… three.'

Sam shuts her eyes as the revolting liquid rushes through her mouth and down her throat. 'Ugh!' She scoops up a handful of crisps, sucking on them to take away the taste.

'Shhh! You'll wake your mum and dad!'

'They're miles away.' Her eyes are watering. She flops down on the sleeping bag, propping herself up with her elbow. 'They went to bed ages ago.' Henry, who has been curled up asleep on the end of the bed, opens one eye, watching her disdainfully.

Greta crunches on a handful of crisps. 'How was that thing at the church tonight?'

'Rubbish. You didn't miss anything.'

'Can I tell you something?'

'Course. What?'

'It's just, when I got home from school today, there was a letter for me. From that woman who does the tea rota at church, Linda Miles.'

'Really?'

'I've only spoken to her, like, twice. The letter - I forgot to bring it - it said she had a message for me, from God. And there's a Bible verse, about darkness and demons or something. It said I'm running away from God - that was it - and he knows I'm suffering and he wants to take away my pain.' Greta laughs, lightly. 'I mean… what do you think?'

'What about?'

'The letter!'

'I don't know.' She screws the lid back on the brandy bottle, tucking it under the pile of clothes at the bottom of her wardrobe to dispose of tomorrow.

When she wakes, the room is pitch black. She sits up, her eyes adjusting to the darkness and shadows. She has kicked the duvet into a heap at the foot of the bed but the heat is still stifling. She lowers her feet to rest on the carpet, stepping carefully around the black silhouette on the floor where Greta is sleeping. She slides back the curtain; the PVC double-glazed window will only open a few inches. She leans across the narrow window sill: even outside, the air is thick, suffocating. All along Trenchard Street, the houses are still and silent.

She feels her way back along the edge of the wardrobe and dressing table to the bed, and lies down, glancing at the luminous arms of the clock on the bedside table: it is five past two. Joe will be home from the meal. She pictures him asleep in his boxer shorts, sprawled out on top of the pale grey duvet in his bedroom. Another image forms in her head of them all sitting around a table in the restaurant, Joe laughing with Kurt and Francesca, Robin and Pippa joining in; Francesca in that striking blue dress.

Joe is really getting on her nerves, going on and on about Kurt. He just won't let it drop: Kurt did this; Kurt said that; 'You should get to know him more, Sam - he's amazing!' And now Joe has been talking to him about her and Greta.

She can hear Greta's faint rhythmic breathing from the dark space beside the bed. That letter from Linda Miles: what was that all about? Joe said everyone knows Greta has problems, didn't he? Everyone is praying for her, he said. Maybe she should have told Greta what Joe said. Why didn't she? She always tells Greta everything. She can still tell her in the morning, she thinks, dubiously.

The aroma of toast wafts through the house. Her father is whistling the tune to 'Shine Your Love' somewhere outside in the garden.

'Good morning.' Her mother takes the tray from her as they enter the kitchen. 'I was looking for that.'

Through the open backdoor, she spots Henry the cat, basking in the sun on the patio.

'Did you sleep all right, Greta?' her mother asks.

'Fine, thanks. Thanks for the pizza.'

'That's all right. You'll have to come and stay again.' Her mother slides squares of warm toast into the metal rack, placing it onto the tray along with a knife, plate, the butter dish, a mug of tea. 'Are you going to the meeting with Sam tonight?'

'I think so.'

'Sam's dad can give you a lift home if you like. He said you're all going with those nice American young people...' Her mother reaches for the jar of Lemon Marmalade from the fridge. 'Oh - before I forget, Sam - Stella phoned to speak to you yesterday, when you were out with Joe. She wanted to know if she could come over after work with your birthday present. I said you'd give her a ring today.'

'Okay.' She hasn't talked to her sister for ages, not since that Sunday when Kurt and Francesca came round for dinner, and then they'd hardly spoken.

'I'll take this out to Dad and we'll see what you girls want for breakfast.'

Twelve

Celebration

'What's that supposed to mean?' Greta says, crossly. 'Not teaching us proper English?'

Maybe she shouldn't have worn jeans tonight, Sam thinks, glancing at her reflection in the window of Habitat. The others will probably all be dressed up. 'They said Mr Allen doesn't teach us enough grammar and stuff. Julia's parents have threatened to send her to a private school sixth form.'

'Thank God!' Greta stamps out the remainder of her cigarette on the pavement. 'I can't believe she actually let her parents complain to the school. It's so embarrassing!'

'I hope Mr. Allen doesn't get into trouble.'

'We could write to Harris anonymously and say what a brilliant teacher he is.'

Sam frowns. 'But what if he finds out *we've* written it? He wouldn't listen to us.'

'We'd have to type it, you idiot, and say it was from a parent.'

She catches sight of their group - Joe, Robin and Pippa, Ben and Avril - waiting with the Americans by the pillars outside the Victoria Rooms. Joe is engaged in conversation with the tall, good looking boy who Kurt was talking to at the party yesterday. Joe phoned this morning to ask her to join him with the Americans in Pizza Hut before the meeting, but she couldn't see the point when she doesn't know any of them.

'Where's Kurt and Francesca?' Robin raises his voice over the chatter.

'And Cindy's not here yet,' the good looking American says, scanning the crowd gathering in the square for their leader.

'I spoke to Kurt on the phone this afternoon.' Joe addresses everyone, importantly. 'He and Cindy are tied up with something. They'll be a bit late – he said not to wait.'

'Okay, well that's all of us then,' Robin beams. 'Shall we go in?'

Their seats are in the stalls, close to the front row where Liz Golding is sitting, her blonde hair standing out among the men in suits.

Sam recognizes her from the glossy photograph on the sleeve of her autobiography; her mother gave her the book to flick through while her father watched the cricket results.

People are filling the rows behind and the balcony above.

'Move along! Move along!' An officious usher in a burgundy uniform patrols up and down the aisles. 'There's a spare seat beside you, madam. People are standing at the back.'

A young man, with flicked, chestnut-brown hair, steps up to the microphone on the stage, smiling. 'Hello, everyone! Welcome to another celebration meeting! I'm Gary, and I'll be leading the praise and worship with you tonight. Let's start with 'Lord, we rejoice in your victory!"

Two young women take their places at the microphone to his side. Behind them, the musicians - the keyboard player, base and electric guitarists, drummer and violinist - begin playing.

Everyone in the hall rises. *'Lord, we rejoice in your victory, Lord, we delight in your love, Lord, we celebrate you've set us free, Lord, you have given us life...'* Their voices resonate through the auditorium. Joe, in a pastel pink v-neck jumper she's never seen before, has the seat in front; his arms are stretched high in praise. Two rows in front, Liz Golding raises her hands. Many have left their chairs and moved to dance in the aisles and by the stage. On the platform, Gary makes a circular dance around the microphone.

'The angels proclaim the splendour of our king; no one can compare with his magnificence. Evermore, he'll be our risen saviour; willingly, I kneel and praise him...'

The musicians play on softly. There is murmuring around the hall, the sound magnifying as members of the audience chant in tongues, praying and shouting. Gary speaks in tongues, rapidly, into the microphone.

A woman's piercing voice rises above the rest from somewhere near the back. 'God is saying to you tonight that he is pleased with you. He delights in your praises! He wants you to give him your whole hearts! To stand together as a mighty army, to march across this city, proclaiming the power of Jesus!'

Sam grips onto the chipped wooden back of Joe's chair. If everyone she knows could be here now, they'd see God, she thinks. They'd have to believe, wouldn't they? She glances to her side: Greta's head is lowered, her blonde hair strewn across her face.

'I fell in love with this dark city,' Liz Golding says. Her accent is foreign: exotic. 'Although I detested the evil and the corruption, I felt compelled to stay. I dreamt of what this place could become: a city without suffering or despair; a city that radiated love. I dreamt of leading the men and women of Hong Kong to the healing power of Jesus.'

Sam tries to picture the gangs of Triads riding motorbikes and living on violence and drugs; hundreds of opium addicts crammed into seedy rooms littered with needles and syringes; the child prostitutes; the stench from the sewers seeping through the streets.

'I was frightened of the sewer rats more than the gangs: my heart went out to them. I had a vision of entering heroin dens, praying for these men and releasing them from their chains. I pictured touching those who were blind and witnessing their sight return.'

All eyes are transfixed on the striking woman on the stage: her long, sun-bleached hair; her startlingly bright blue eyes; her glowing skin. It's no wonder that she's shown thousands to God, Sam thinks: anyone can see the power of God in her, his light.

'Before I finish tonight, I want to say a few words about God's gift of tongues. It is through this gift that God has given me the power to perform miracles. Opium addicts have been cured instantly and found Jesus, and spoken themselves in God's holy language. If any of you here have not yet experienced this gift yourself, I urge you to receive his healing power before you leave here tonight.'

Gary and the backing singers return quietly to their places on the stage. The musicians begin playing softly; *'We embrace you, Holy Spirit; we embrace you, Holy Spirit! Bring us your holy fire as we surrender all worldly desires, our souls reaching out for you. We embrace you, Holy Spirit; Holy Spirit, we embrace you!'*

'I'd like to invite any of you who want to be filled with the Holy Spirit tonight,' Gary says into the microphone, 'to come up onto the platform now, and Liz and her team will pray for you.'

The music and singing continue quietly while people negotiate their way across the building to the front. *'We embrace you, Holy Spirit; we embrace you, Holy Spirit! Let your presence move through us; let us walk in the Spirit's flow. We embrace you, Holy Spirit; Holy Spirit, we embrace you!'*

Greta nudges her out of her daze. 'I'm going up.'

She watches her friend's blue satin shirt and blonde hair swish up the steps to the stage. Liz Golding and the men in suits move from person to person, talking in hushed voices, praying over them. Around the auditorium, groups are moving from their seats to leave. She glances at her watch: the meeting has run over time.

Joe swivels around, leaning over the back of the chair. 'It's great, isn't it?' He beams towards the front, where Greta has vanished out of sight. 'I knew God would answer our prayers.'

'Yeah.' The Spirit is on the stage and she wishes she were up there too, with Greta.

'I've got to go,' Joe says. 'I'm getting a lift back with Robin. You all right waiting on your own?'

'Course. My dad'll be here in a minute.'

The musicians carry out equipment. Men in uniforms are closing up the exits at the sides of the hall and checking between the rows of seats. Everyone from the youth group has gone. Sam moves to stand at the back of the auditorium. On the platform, there is still a group of people waiting to be prayed for. Greta is nowhere to be seen.

Am I really filled with the Holy Spirit, she wonders? If I am, then why do I feel like this? She checks her watch again: half past eleven. Her father will be waiting in the car.

Greta appears suddenly, waving from the steps. As she draws near, Sam senses something is wrong. 'What happened?'

Greta looks utterly dismayed. 'She didn't have time to pray for me.'

'It doesn't matter... You can get filled with the Holy Spirit anytime, can't you?'

Thirteen

Faith

Her father drives the Escort slowly away from Greta's house. 'It's very late. Is she all right on her own?'

From the passenger window, Sam watches the house light up: the hallway, the living room. 'Her Gran only lives two doors down.'

'Should we have taken her there?'

'She'd rather be in her own house.'

'You can always ask her to stay with us.'

'I know.'

Marine Road is deserted; the sea, to their right, is a black endless space. Her father's profile is illuminated by the street lamps: his ruffled greying hair; the pale freckled skin on his arms and hands.

He turns the wheel, steering the car into Portland Street. 'The meeting went on late.'

'Mm.'

'Was it good?'

'Yeah.'

'Did Kurt bring the American young people?'

'The Americans came, but I don't think Kurt and Francesca were there.'

'That's strange. They were at the party last night, and they went out for a meal afterwards with...' She senses him glance at her as he turns into Trenchard Street. 'I'm sorry, love. Joe should have taken you along with him.'

Her mum must have said something to him. 'It doesn't matter.' She stares through the windscreen at the row of silent houses.

The car pulls into the driveway; she slips off her seatbelt. All of the rooms are in darkness except for the lamp in the porch. Her father lets them into the hallway, flicking on the lights.

She heads straight for the stairs.

'Aren't you having any supper?' In the past, when he's brought her home late at night, they've shared mugs of hot chocolate and hot buttered toast, and sat at the kitchen table and talked.

'No, I'm all right.'

She can see he's relieved to go to bed; he's speaking in the morning service.

She plumps the pillows up against the pink velvet headboard and sits cross-legged on top of the duvet. Henry, curled at the end of the bed, watches her through half-closed eyelids.

The mountain of exercise books, text books, revision guides on her desk needs sorting out; she should do that tomorrow, she thinks, and she must do something about her room. When they moved here, she chose the pastel pink walls, the Liberty floral duvet cover and matching curtains, the rose-coloured carpet. Now it is too pink and babyish. Her old fluffy toys, given to her as birthday and Christmas gifts, year after year, for as long as she can remember, are piled in a heap in the corner; her Sindy dolls - one with yellow hair and the other brunette - are still propped on the shelf above the desk, along with the white plastic Sindy dressing table and wardrobe. Tomorrow she will definitely move those. When Francesca came round that time, at least she didn't come in here. It would have been *so* embarrassing.

She's wide awake, her mind flicking through image after image: Joe sitting on Kurt and Francesca's new settee at their house in Portishead, discussing her; Francesca's hands on her shoulders on the residential; Greta's crestfallen face on the platform steps tonight. If only Francesca had been there to help. She said she was going; where was she? She hopes she's all right. She looked fine last night.

It's all becoming clear, what she must do. Soon everyone will be able to see she's right with God, she's filled with the Holy Spirit.

She closes her eyes, concentrating. 'Dear God...' Carefully, she chooses the right words. 'Please forgive me for failing over the past few months. I'm going to be more committed. I'll pray more and read the Bible every day, and try to make my praise in the meetings more meaningful. Help me move forward with my faith, and speak to me powerfully through the Holy Spirit. Amen.'

She blinks in the hazy glow from the bedside lamp. The room is utterly still. Henry is motionless on the end of the bed, his head tucked between his paws. She understands now: if she gets herself right with God, everything else will fall into place. She reaches for the brass clock on the bedside table. Tomorrow she will get up early and make a new start.

She wakes with a jump to the shrill ring of the alarm bell. Then she remembers: it's Sunday and she doesn't have to go to school.

Her bare feet move soundlessly across the beige landing carpet and down the stairway.

'Sam!' Her father is sitting at the kitchen table, pouring over a book, piles of papers ordered neatly around him. He removes his reading glasses. 'You made me jump. What're you doing up?'

She has forgotten that he rises early on Sundays to look over his sermon. 'I just felt like it.'

He smiles. 'I know what you mean. This is the best time of the day.'

'D'you want a cup of tea?' she offers.

'Yes, thank you.'

Her father becomes absorbed in reading once more as she makes two mugs of tea, refills Henry's water dish and biscuit bowl.

In her room, she sits on the carpet, leaning her back against the edge of the bed. She closes her eyes. 'Thank you God, for everything you've done for me,' she says, silently in her head. 'I pray for Greta, that she will turn to you and let you into her life more... And my GCSE's: please help me to do well and get really good grades.' She pauses; a woodpigeon is cooing outside the window. 'Lord, please speak to me now about the changes you want me to make in my life. Let your Spirit work through me in whatever I do.'

Fourteen

Prayer

'Are you sure your mum won't be back?'

'Not 'til four.' Greta hands her a glass of Cream Soda, fizzing with Neapolitan ice cream, and flops down beside her on the beach towel. 'She does singing lessons on Tuesdays.'

It was easy to slip out of the school gate, across Springfield Road, to the footpath behind Marine Road. 'D'you think we could get in trouble?'

'No-one saw us. We're not missing anything anyway. Mr May will only be making everyone fill in more bloody questionnaires. He's such a waste of time!'

Mr May was appointed by Clevedon High this term, joining Mrs May in the French department. Mrs May told them that her husband would be organising some useful French speaking practice before their oral exam.

'As part of my Masters in Education, I'm practising a new, experimental way of teaching,' he'd said to their class, speaking tediously slowly and gesturing excessively with his hands. '*You*, J5, are going to be part of my research.'

For the last two of Mr May's Tuesday afternoon lessons, they were asked to discuss their preferred learning methods, writing their ideas down on his questionnaires, while he leant casually on the edge of his desk, hands in the pockets of his navy cords, chatting with Heidi and Tamsin, who look like models with their waist-length glossy hair.

'It's not fair! So many teachers are couples: Mr and Mrs Pike, Mr and Mrs Yates, and now Mr and Mrs May.' Greta flips onto her side, propping herself up with her elbow. 'Married people shouldn't be allowed to work in the same school. If one of them doesn't like you, they're bound to talk, and then they'll both hate you.'

'They don't hate you.' Sam shields her eyes with her hand. 'They just haven't realized you're good at French.'

'Because we don't speak any French! That's what we should be doing. Not stupid discussions, in English!' Greta sits up, reaching for the upside-down plant pot where she's placed her packet of Embassy No 1 and the radio. She twists the dial; Radio 1 is playing Whitney

Houston: 'I wanna dance with somebody'. 'Those shorts suit you!'

She squints down at the bright red and green striped shorts she's borrowed from Greta. 'Could you make *me* a pair? After the exams?'

'Remind me. There's loads of material left.'

'Thanks.' She pushes her fringe away from her eyes: it's unbearably heavy in this heat. 'It's two weeks until my next haircut.'

'You'd look great with short hair.'

'That's all right for you to say.' She glances at Greta's long, thick hair; she can still see the streak of purple over which Mrs Twist hauled her into the office two weeks ago. 'I thought I might have it a bit shorter, and layered.'

Greta pulls her Zippo from her pocket and reaches for her cigarettes. 'Want one?' She offers the white packet to Sam.

'No, I'm okay.'

'You didn't finish what you were saying before.' Greta inhales, lighting a cigarette.

'What?'

'Which boy would you most like to spend an evening with?'

She picks up her glass of Cream Soda, slurping on the ice cream still fizzing at the top. 'I'm not sure... I suppose it would have to be Joe, or Mr Allen. Mr Allen would be better but not if he was still my teacher. That'd be so embarrassing! What about you?'

Greta sighs, dramatically, exhaling a long trail of smoke. 'That's the problem. There's no-one... unless I was totally desperate.'

'What about Jack O'Connor?' She giggles.

Greta pulls a face. 'He's just a child!'

'Colin Patterson?' Colin is one of the sixth formers who came to Christian Union last Friday. He moved his chair to their end of the table and talked non-stop all the way through the meeting. No-one could get a word in edgeways.

Greta looks appalled. 'Colin Patterson? Give me *some* credit. He wears white trainers, for God's sake. I mean, would *you* fancy him?'

She laughs, picturing Colin: his mop of carrot-orange hair; his yellowish skin; his arms, covered with masses of freckles and ginger hairs. 'He *is* gross! Greta, we ought to be going back soon... I was thinking, what if Mr May sees us going into school?'

'It's stupid going back, when school's finished.'

'But we promised Francesca. You are coming, aren't you?'

'Who else is going?'

She shrugs. 'Come on, it's the first one. We can't let Francesca down.'

The conference room is light and airy. Francesca looks incredible, dressed in a crisp white, sleeveless shirt accentuating her slim, tanned arms. 'Hi, girls! What a gorgeous day! You've caught the sun, Greta.'

'Have I?' Greta touches her scarlet nose.

Julia Lamb is already present, and Sarah McIvor, Maria Davies, Noel Stewart, Colin Patterson. They pile coats and school bags onto the long wooden table and help Francesca move the chairs into a circle by the open window. Colin somehow manages to edge his chair between hers and Greta's.

'Thanks for bringing along your guitar, Colin,' Francesca smiles, politely, 'but I don't think there'll be time to sing as well as pray.'

Thank goodness, she thinks, imagining having to sing here with so few of them.

Francesca passes around photocopies of the prayer list. 'I'd like us to pray for a new group, Christians United in Schools. It's been set up by two young men, Phil and John; they're trying to build bridges between Christian Unions in schools across Bristol. I had a meeting with them yesterday and I've said to Phil we'd like to get involved as much as possible.' She glances warmly in Sam's direction.

There are nods of agreement around the circle.

Francesca slides her finger down the list, thoughtfully. 'You'll see I've put down 'Assemblies'. The headmaster asked me if we'll take the second year assembly next month. It's a great opportunity to make a stand for what we believe in. And...,' she looks up, 'lastly, Noel's asked if we'll pray for Jason Jones. He came to the first Jigsaw meeting, if you remember, but apparently he's been suspended from school. Does anyone know what happened?'

They can all imagine the reasons. Jason has started hanging out with the lads who park their cars outside Tesco's in the evenings, who wheel spin around the car park, shrieking at passers-by. The thump of their stereos can be heard streets away. Whenever Sam walks past, girls are draped over the boys, swigging from cans and staggering about.

Francesca looks concerned. 'Have any of you heard from him?'

'I saw him in the shopping precinct at the weekend,' Maria says. 'He was smoking and drinking. I asked him if he was coming to CU again and he said he felt too bad at the moment.'

Francesca's composure remains calm. 'Okay, we'll pray for Jason, shall we?'

On the other side of the circle, Noel and Maria nod gravely.

'Does anybody have anything else they'd like us to pray about?' Francesca moves her gaze around the group.

'My GCSE exams,' Julia Lamb says, in a whiny voice. 'I'm worried about revising.'

Francesca makes a note on her list.

'It's not just *her* who's got exams,' Greta chips in. 'We've *all* got our exams coming up in a few weeks.'

'Have you? We must pray you'll all do well then.'

'I'd like to pray for Sally, too,' Sarah adds, quickly. 'She's not talking to me again.'

Sally Scott and Sarah are meant to be best friends but Sally is always ignoring her or storming off.

Francesca turns to Maria. 'Sally goes to the Methodist youth group with you sometimes, doesn't she?'

Maria nods. 'She's the same there. She acts funny.'

'Does anyone know what's wrong?' Francesca glances around the circle again. 'Any problems at home?'

'She was upset yesterday at lunchtime,' Sarah confides, quietly. 'She's not allowed to go out or have anyone round, and she cries every night.'

Sam risks a quick look at Greta, who rolls her eyes.

'She does go out,' Maria interrupts, 'with Nathan from the Methodist group.'

'You think that might be one of the problems?' Francesca asks. 'Her boyfriend?'

'I thought they'd finished. That's what she told me.' The red patch on Sarah's neck is slowly rising. 'Because he wanted to have sex with her.'

'Oh dear!' Francesca sighs, running her tanned fingers across her forehead. 'Well, let's pray for Sally too.'

Francesca leans back in her chair and lowers her eyelids. She looks perfectly beautiful, Sam thinks.

Behind her eyelids is deep red space. She tries to shut out Maria breathing noisily beside her, the smell of lemon polish.

'Lord, I pray for Sally. Show me the right thing to do and say. I pray she'll know that, through you, she can always be happy. Amen.'

'Father, we pray for Jason.' Francesca's voice is soft and low. 'He's drifted away from the things of you. Lord, we know that if our walk with you becomes weak, we become vulnerable to the world and sin can creep in. We pray that Jason will feel able to come to the meetings again and find your forgiveness and love. Amen.'

Sam takes a deep breath. 'Lord, we pray for the GCSE exams. We know you'll always take care of us. We can rely on you completely and let you support us. Amen.'

She is different to the others who go to the Baptist Church and the Methodist Church, she thinks; she has the Holy Spirit with her, doesn't she? Only Francesca truly understands. She can sense the Spirit, in the space under her ribs, like an invisible thread joining them together.

Fifteen

The Bible

The phone rings loudly from the shelf beside the dining table, where she is reading the fat yellow Maths workbook. She places the book face down to keep her place and picks up the receiver: 'Hello?'

'Hi, it's me.'

'Hi Joe.'

'D'you want to meet in Bristol?'

'I've just started some revision.'

'You're off on half term, aren't you? You've got all week to do that.'

'I haven't. I'm going to Brighton on Monday, remember?'

'Oh yeah! With Greta. Thanks a lot!'

'Hold on. Remember what happened last time you came with me to Brighton, when you were sick on the coach home after the trifle. You said you were never going again. And anyway, you know Greta doesn't have proper holidays.'

'What about today then? I've not seen you for ages.'

'You've normally got things to do.' She picks up the pencil she has just sharpened and begins drawing loops along the edge of the squared paper. 'How's Kurt?'

'He's having some time out with Francesca. They've gone to stay overnight in a hotel by the sea or something.'

'That's romantic.'

'It's for Francesca; Kurt says she's still struggling settling in.'

'She doesn't look like it. Are you sure?'

'Of course I am. Kurt's doing everything he can to help her feel better.'

'Did you ask why they didn't come to the celebration?'

'He said something about it being difficult with Cindy staying.'

'The American youth leader?'

'Yeah. I don't know... Are you going to meet me then? We could get a video out.'

On the other side of the double glazed window, the midday sun is already strong. 'I can't, Joe. My first Maths exam's the day after half term. You could come back for lunch after church tomorrow if you want.'

'It's music group practice.'

'I forgot about that. I'll see you in church anyway.'

Once she's replaced the receiver, her mother opens the door. 'Fancy a break, love? I'm just popping round to see Stella.'

'I've hardly done anything.' She eyes the impossibly thick workbook.

'It's a lovely day. It'll only be a couple of hours.'

Her mother parks the Mini in Woodland Terrace, across the road from the Victorian terraced house where Stella lives. Sam's only been here once before; on the day Stella moved in, she came over with her father to help paint the living room. Her father wouldn't trust her with a paintbrush so she'd spent all afternoon unwrapping sheets of newspaper from Stella's crockery and ornaments.

She presses the buzzer for flat two; her sister's voice crackles through the intercom: 'Come in!'

They traipse up the flight of stairs, through Stella's front door into the living room at the front of the house. Neatly framed pictures are now hanging from the magnolia walls: Van Gogh's Sunflowers, an abstract of red and pink squares.

'Tea or coffee?' asks Stella, heading towards the kitchen across the hallway.

Her mother follows. 'A cup of tea thanks, love.'

'Sam?' Stella calls.

'I'll have tea.' She takes a seat on the settee. The tree-lined street outside the wide bay window is quiet. You'd never know that the bustle of Whiteladies Road, where her sister used to live, was just around the corner. Stella's old house was shared with three friends - Mo, Imogen and Dan - who were nice, but the house was always so chaotic whenever she went round that she never stayed long.

She runs her eyes over the room. Stella is tidy, like all of them in her family; everything is put away in its place, except for the pile of cassette tapes left on the carpet beside the stereo, a black leather handbag on the armchair. The surfaces of the sideboard are empty; there's just a bottle of something - Bailey's - left out on the shelf. There's nothing on the coffee table either, except a neat stack of square cork coasters and a small black book, worn at the edges. She picks it up, opening the cover: an address book; cards and scraps of paper scatter across the beige carpet. She hastily gathers them up and tucks them back inside, replacing it on the table.

Then she notices a torn slip of paper lying on the carpet by the window; it must have flown off from the others. She stoops to pick it up, noticing the word 'STELLA', scrawled in capital letters. She unfolds the note; she shouldn't, she thinks.

'Meet you at 6,' she reads. 'There's so much I want to know about you.' There's no name.

She refolds the paper and shoves it guiltily inside the cover of the address book. Her sister has never mentioned a boyfriend or anything. Stella never says much about herself at all. She hasn't come to the services for years, she thinks. Does that mean that she doesn't believe in God? Nobody ever mentions her at church and her parents never speak about why she doesn't come. Perhaps she could be the one to help her. She'll pray for her, she decides.

Stella sets the mugs of tea down on the coasters, pushing back the blonde curl that has fallen in front of her eyes with a sweep of her pale fingers. Her bobbed hair is thick and wavy, similar to her father's.

Sam leans back against the settee cushions. 'It's nice in here.'

'I like it. I'm not keen on the furniture but at least it's my own place.'

'How's work, Stella?' their mother asks.

'Busy. You remember Jon, who does publicity? His wife's had a baby so he's been off this week and I'm having to pick up some of his stuff. It's just extra work, that's all.'

'Oh dear.'

'Only one more week before I'm on that plane to Paris.' Stella smiles over to her. 'Mum said you're off on half term this week.'

'Yeah, I'm going to Grandma's with Greta.'

'Blimey, that's brave!'

'They're all right.'

'Your Grandma always asks after you, Stella,' their mother chips in.

'Mm. When're you back, Sam?'

'Friday.'

'Well, why don't we go out next Saturday, like we used to?'

When Stella had lived at home, she'd take her to the watch the kids' matinees at The Curzon on Saturdays, or for cakes in Sandra's Tearoom. 'Okay.'

'Before I forget...' Her sister crosses the room, opening the sideboard drawer. 'Happy birthday.' She hands Sam a narrow white envelope. 'Sorry it's late.'

She tears open the seal: inside is a card holding three ten pound book vouchers.

'I didn't know what to get. Mum said you've always got your head in a book.'

'That's great! Thanks!'

Music is playing softly across the shop: '*As the desert waits for rainfall, my heart yearns after you. You are everything I long for...*' She cradles the gold cardboard box containing the precious leather-bound book.

'Are you sure, Sam?' her mother asks 'No-one reads the Amplified Bible these days.'

'Kurt said it's the truest Bible.'

'Well I don't know why he should say that. It uses five words for every one in the Good News.'

'The Good News Bible's for children.'

Her mother picks up a hardback book with an image of a sunrise on the cover, 'What about the New International version? It's much more modern, and easier to understand.'

'But I want this one. I can use my vouchers.' She carries the gold box over to the cash till.

'*You're my helper and you're my companion; I adore you more than anything...*' She recognises the song, she thinks; didn't Megan Morris sing it in church? She glances at the shelves of books, cassettes, cards, stickers, bookmarks. She'd like to spend longer looking around properly, but not now, with her mother interfering. She'll bring Greta, next time they come shopping in Park Street.

Sixteen

Cleansed

Sam tugs back the floral curtains and pushes the window ajar. The sky is already blue, the street still, except for the rustle of the wind brushing through the willow trees across the street.

She sits cross-legged on the pink carpet, leaning against the edge of the bed, ignoring the stack of books still piled on top of her desk. She'll write a revision plan later, complete some past exam papers. She must make the most of this morning; it won't be easy to find time on her own with God once she's in Brighton with Greta.

She closes her eyes and lets her mind become still. A dog is barking from the garden at number 17. Henry pads across the carpet and jumps onto the windowsill.

'Dear God, please help me in my GCSE exams. I know I never have to worry about anything because you're in control and you have a wonderful plan for my life. And I pray for Greta; please give me a chance to talk to her when we're on holiday next week. Show me a way to help her.'

Her sister keeps coming into her thoughts. It'll be strange meeting her next week, she thinks; she can't remember the last time they did anything like that. 'Dear God..., please give me the chance to talk to Stella about you.'

She turns to the contents page of *Moving Deeper*, the guide that Teresa - her tent leader from last year's summer camp - gave her, choosing a chapter, 'A Powerful Friend.'

'As we spend time before God each day,' she reads, 'to give him our praises, read his word and let him speak into our lives, it will be like adding paraffin to the flame that God has lit in our hearts. The flame will spread to a raging fire and our faith and courage will increase. God will then be able to shine through us and use us mightily as servants in this city and in our nation.'

She slips her new Bible from the box, inhaling the leathery smell as she opens the cover, turning the gold-rimmed, tissue paper pages, running her eyes over the fine script. Last night, she began underlining sections with a ruler, writing neat annotations in the margins. Kurt's and Francesca's Bibles are covered in writing.

She shuts her eyes and flicks through the pages. 'Lord, please speak to me now. Show me what I need to understand.' She places her hand on the page that falls open; her finger rests on a verse from Proverbs: 'Trust in the Lord with all your heart and lean not on your own understanding; in all your ways acknowledge him, and he will direct your paths.'

'Trust God in everything,' she notes in the margin. 'Be open for him to guide me.'

She can pick out Joe's bass guitar amidst the sounds of the violin, the flute, the keyboard and drums. She hasn't said anything to him about what's happened to her. She isn't going to tell anyone; she'll wait until they notice how different she is. So many things have changed already. The services are the only place where she can completely be herself; other things seem quite pointless compared to what truly matters.

The museum is ecstatic with praise. Hands are raised high in the air; men in suits and women in their Sunday dresses dance in the aisles. That's something that she still can't do, she thinks: her legs are like lead weights.

It was the same on the residential weekend last year when John and Rachel Fisher ran the youth group. 'Dancing is a powerful way for women to express their praises to God', John told them, and all the girls had to accompany Pippa, who was always John's favourite, into the crypt to learn the dance moves to an Amy Grant song, 'Time to Fly', to perform in front of the entire congregation the following morning. Pippa was graceful; Sam awkward; Greta refused to do it.

'*Lord God, you sent your son to tear down Satan's works. Jesus has overcome! So with joy we lift our voices...*' Arlene Hartley, standing next to her, is an enthusiastic singer. Sam's voice blends in with all the others and she can't, thankfully, hear herself, which means that Greta, on her other side, can't either.

The youth group, under Kurt's instructions, now sit amongst the body of the congregation; only the gang from Light of the World, the drug rehabilitation centre affiliated to their church, still occupy the back row. Tim, one of the elders, co-ordinates the programme, bringing the minibus of rough-looking young men to the Sunday services. Most have been addicted to heroin and need God to change their lives. The group is transient: there are always new arrivals, who soon find God, and those who appear in church one week, giving harrowing testimonies at the front, then simply vanish, never to be seen again.

The musicians play softly; across the museum, members of the congregation murmur prayers, speaking in tongues and quietly singing. Francesca, in the row in front, is bathed in a strip of sunlight from the arched window. Sam gazes at her lowered eyelids; her olive skin; her hair falling lightly over her shoulders, dark against her white dress.

She senses the Spirit brush against her skin as it moves through the room. A sharp voice penetrates above the others as Adele Thomas, seated by the stained glass window on the other side of the hall, rises and breaks into the holy language: harsh shrill words reverberating around the stone walls. The room quietens as the congregation wait for God to give someone the interpretation.

Malcolm Bradley, by the pillar at the back, stands. 'God is saying to you this morning, my people, sing your praises to me with pure hearts. You are burdened with the chains of sin.' His voice is sombre. 'He asks you to seek his forgiveness this morning and cleanse yourselves. God wants you to be pure, so that you might come freely into his presence.'

Silence permeates the hall.

'To take communion in an impure state is a sin.' Pastor Loveday gazes across the congregation. 'And as you all know, sins include unholy thoughts as well as deeds. Before you take the holy communion this morning, each of you must empty yourselves of your own sinful nature so that God can wash you clean and fill you with his spirit.'

She searches herself for every impure thing she might have done. 'God, please forgive me for thinking of myself instead of you; for all the times in the past I could have been praying and doing more for you; ... for the things that happened between Joe and me, that I know we shouldn't have done. Lord, please take these things away and cleanse me.'

'*You gave your life for me,*' the congregation sing, while the bread and wine is passed from row to row. '*You gave your blood to cleanse me, as clear as water from the spring …*'

The thick, heavy feeling in her body is lifting. The Holy Spirit washes through her until she is light and pure, a clean white space.

Greta passes her the basket and she takes a piece of bread, resting the white square on her tongue.

Arlene Hartley's eyes are shut tightly; Sam taps the spongy satin shoulder of her dress and holds out the basket. Arlene beams at her lovingly.

Greta hands her the tray holding the silver cups of wine; not real wine: it is red and sweet, leaving a metallic taste on her tongue. The miniature cups are new, introduced for hygiene reasons, she heard her mother say to Evelyn Winstanley. They used to pass around a silver goblet and a cotton napkin, each person taking a sip and wiping the rim with the napkin. She'd never liked the idea of putting her mouth where Veronica Neal's had been.

Greta has vanished outside for a cigarette by herself; that is, not exactly on her own: with Irish Adam, from Light of the World. It is accepted that the drug rehabilitation lot are allowed to wear scruffy jeans and denim jackets, and smoke outside the glass museum doors on Sunday mornings. They've gone through enough giving up heroin; other minor issues need not be addressed until later in their paths.

Last Sunday, when Greta slipped out for an after-service cigarette, Adam, apparently, offered to accompany her. Greta told her that Adam was addicted to heroin and a heavy drinker in Ireland, but he's completely clean now. He smiled and winked at Greta by the entrance this morning, Sam noticed.

'Hey there!' A heavy hand grips her shoulder.

She spins around. 'Hello,' she replies, meekly.

'You must be worried, right?'

'Sorry?' Kurt is standing too close.

'About your friend. You must be concerned about her.'

'Well-'

'I understand. We must give it to God; he'll always find a way.'

'Yeah, okay.'

He smiles, knowingly. 'Joe's a lucky guy.'

She turns towards the platform where Joe is talking to Lucy Longthorn, the flute player.

Kurt winks. 'I hope he's behaving himself.'

Kurt's roar of a laugh prompts her to take another glance at Joe: he hasn't even noticed she's still here.

Seventeen

Gospel

'There it is!' Sam waves in the direction of the bright yellow camper van parked at the other end of Seaview Terrace, the red cross, that lights up in the dark, suspended prominently above the front windscreen.

'THE WAGES OF SIN ARE DEATH.' Greta reads the black text plastered along the van's side and laughs.

'It's not funny! Someone complained about it last time they stayed with us.'

'What happened?'

'They pushed a note through our letterbox saying it was offensive.'

'Who was it?'

'One of the neighbours, I s'pose. There wasn't a name.'

'Hello, dear.' Her grandmother squeezes her tightly against the scratchy fabric of her lilac knitted dress. 'Haven't you grown tall? Is this your friend?'

Nothing has changed. In the living room, there's the Grandfather clock that chimes at seven and thirty-seven minutes past each hour; the ornament cabinet displaying the orange dogs, pink ducks, and china cups and saucers that Gran never uses; the out of tune piano stacked with frayed hymn books. The centrepiece of the room still hangs above the fireplace: an evocative painting of the Second Coming, the red fires of damnation sweeping over a city; the sky full of billowing smoke, angels blowing gold trumpets and hundreds of tiny people who've been driving along in their cars or walking in the park, and dogs, leaving the ground and ascending towards heaven. Someone, she notices, has added a sticker to the corner with the words 'PERHAPS TODAY'.

'Come and see your room,' Gran says.

They troop after her up the narrow stairs to the front bedroom.

'You can see the sea from here.' Sam jumps onto the green candlewick bedspread, craning to see the strip of blue over the rooftops.

The room is exactly the same as it was when she spent her summer holidays here as a child: the lime patterns in the wallpaper looping like bass clefs; in the corner, the cot piled with blankets, teddy bears, a plastic doll with a pink ribbon in her hair; over the cot, the picture of the little boy with large blue eyes and snowy white pyjamas, kneeling, his hands clasped in prayer; the dressing table mirror covered in battered stickers – 'God is love' and 'God is my castle' (with a cartoon picture of a sandcastle) - that she and Stella were given at the beach mission.

'You must watch the video!' Gran leads them downstairs to the front room, the best room, in which nobody usually sits.

She thought that her grandparents disapproved of the television. Her family always laugh at the tale of one being delivered once by mistake, with 'Bringing the world to your home' printed on the side of the cardboard box: Grandad had sent it straight back. When her grandparents visit her house, her father swings the 'hellevision' around to face the wall in the corner of the living room.

The front room has been redecorated with a wall-sized poster of the Swiss Alps. Her grandmother has made additions to the pine trees: seagulls, budgies, parrots and robin redbreasts, snipped out of old birthday and Christmas cards. The floral three-piece-suite now faces the new television set.

Her grandmother slips the video tape into the recorder: on the T.V. screen appears a clip of the inside of a pub, and there are her grandparents and their group - Muriel, Queenie and Ethel - lined up in front of the bar. They are wearing the orange and yellow luminous gospel jackets that Grandad made, with 'THE END IS NIGH' printed down the fronts; Queenie is quoting from the Old Testament into the microphone. This is followed by singing led by Grandad and Ethel, Gran and Muriel on accordions, Queenie jigging and waving a tambourine. Customers are squeezing past them to reach the bar.

'Look at us with all them boozers!' Gran, on the edge of the armchair, chuckles. 'The mockers and the scoffers!'

Meanwhile, Arthur, the camera man, zooms in on sinners' faces and pint glasses in people's hands.

Beside the pier, a group of toddlers and their mothers are kneeling on the pavement in front of the Punch and Judy show.

'Your gran and grandad are bonkers!' Greta grins.

'I know.' Greta's grandparents are totally different, she thinks: her grandad smokes Camel cigarettes and spends his evenings sitting at the bar in The Wagon and Horses.

'Can you believe those jackets!'

'I wore one once.'

Greta hoots. 'You didn't!'

'When I was going out with Justin. Remember him?'

Greta giggles.

'He came on holiday with us and we went to Brighton market with Grandad. We had to wear the jackets and go up to people on the streets and give them leaflets.'

'Oh no!'

'Grandad gave us a load of tracts to take home. We spent weeks putting them through letter boxes and inside magazines in Smiths.'

Greta clutches her stomach. 'Don't tell me anymore!'

They head away from the noise, past the ice cream stalls; the warm, sticky smells of doughnuts and candyfloss; the row of pastel-painted Victorian hotels lining the promenade. Taking off their baseball boots, they cross the beach to where the sand is damp and flat. When she was younger, they would all troop down here: her parents and Stella, Gran and Grandad, with deckchairs, buckets and spades, Grandad in the grey suit he always wore, only taking off his shoes and socks and rolling up his trousers, revealing white bony ankles, when the heat was blistering.

'What's Joe doing this week?' Greta asks.

'No idea. Probably helping Kurt with something or other.'

'Didn't you hear Kurt say at the meeting? He's going on a men's training course for ministers speaking at that festival.'

'That's right.' The Festival of Light is taking place in the summer holidays, at a Happy Parks site in Southaven. Most of their church are going, along with thousands of Christians from all over the country.

'I'm surprised Joe hasn't gone with him, since he's such a big star. Francesca won't be there, will she, if it's for men?'

'Maybe they let wives go too.'

Greta pulls out her white packet of Embassy No.1 and lights a cigarette. 'Is everything all right with Joe?'

'...It's been funny the last few weeks.'

'How d'you mean?'

'I don't know... What about you and that guy, Adam?'

Greta rubs her forehead. 'He's great; you should talk to him. He's not allowed to go out with anyone, though. Not until he's finished his programme, and that's eight months away.'

'At least he won't stop you revising.'

'Oh God!'

'We have to do some this week, okay? Why don't we work in the mornings and then we can have the rest of the day off?'

Greta exhales a long plume of smoke. 'But we're on holiday!'

'It's important!'

'You sound like Mrs Twist.'

Sam shoves her. 'I don't! You have brought some work with you, haven't you?'

Greta laughs, turning towards the sea. 'Come on - I want to paddle.'

She helps to clear the leftover ham sandwiches, mince tarts, coconut cakes and trifle from the table.

'Have some more pop,' Grandad says, 'and some nice peaches and vanilla ice-cream to finish. I bought it special.'

'We've had enough to eat, Grandad. Honest.'

Her grandfather settles himself on the armchair; her grandmother draws the curtains and seats herself between Sam and Greta on the lumpy settee, her feet propped on the pouf, toes poking through the holes in her tan tights.

'I have twenty-five grandchildren,' Gran turns to Greta, 'and they all love Jesus.'

'That's great!' Greta replies, cheerily. She seems to be getting used to them.

Sam picks up the biscuit tin; the yellow roses on the side have faded, the lid full of dents. 'What're you having, Grandad? Rich Tea or a Digestive?'

Her grandmother pats her hand and hooks her other arm through Greta's. 'Now, Greta dear, your mum and dad don't go to the church, do they?'

'Er, no.'

'You need to be telling them about Jesus before it's too late. If they don't find the Lord, they'll go to hell.'

Grandad dunks a digestive biscuit into his tea.

Greta bites her lip and frowns.

Sam yawns. 'We're really tired, Gran. We'd better get to bed; we're getting up early to revise.'

She and Greta escape upstairs, where the only thing to do is lie on the candlewick bedspread and play Scrabble.

Eighteen

The path of darkness

'D'you want toast?' Greta calls up the stairs.

'Yeah. Be down in a minute.' She tugs the brush through her hair, stooping to peer at her reflection in the mirror, positioned at Gran's height, above the mantelpiece.

There are dark shadows under her eyes; last night she awoke at two and couldn't get back to sleep. She's slept badly all week on her grandmother's ancient mattress.

She lifts the yellowing net curtain, tying it in a knot, revealing the scaffolding erected by the council at the front of the house. Her grandmother will come in later, tutting, and replace the curtain back across the window. There is a pocket Bible on the window ledge, she notices, with a picture of the three kings on the cover; it wasn't there yesterday. Placed next to the Bible is a leaflet headed 'How To Search For God'.

Her own precious Bible is still lying in its box, neglected, at the bottom of the blue suitcase; she's not had chance to read it since they arrived. She has prayed every night in her head, after she and Greta finish talking and switch the light off, but it's not the same. At least tonight she'll be back in her own bedroom where she can be alone again with God.

'Have the workmen finished?' she asks Gran, entering the kitchen.

'Oh yes. I'm glad they've gone.' Her grandmother and Greta are sitting at the small kitchen table eating hot buttered toast with mugs of milky tea. Gran's hair is still tied in rags. 'I couldn't even make a cup of tea in peace. I opened the kitchen curtains in the mornings and there'd be two legs at the window. In the sitting room, there'd be another pair of legs at that window, and in the front room, you'd see them all out there, waving at me. I don't know what Molly thought.'

'Molly?'

'Molly, the seagull. She sits in the garden every morning.'

Greta lets out a giggle.

Sam places the miniature Bible, from the bedroom, on the table and flicks open the book to the middle of the Psalms, where a small circular mirror has been jammed into the pages; some of the pages have been ripped to make a neat fit. 'Gran, what's this?'

'So I can see if my hat's on straight, of course. It's always slipping in church. I've asked our Rose to get some lipstick an' all, something that'll look pretty when I go to my grandchildren's weddings.'

'Who's getting married?'

'Stella's the oldest, isn't she?'

'But she's not even got a boyfriend!'

Grandad is chuckling in the living room. 'Your gran just wants to buy a new hat.'

'God's got someone for everyone.' Gran nods, wisely. 'She's better waiting for the right one. I waited for the war to end before I married your grandad.'

Sam helps herself to a soggy slice of toast. 'Why don't we get you some shopping before we go? Our train doesn't leave 'til two.'

'That's nice, but don't get chicken, will you, dear? Your Auntie Denise gives me chicken. At your Auntie Trisha's, we had chicken for lunch, chicken for tea, and when your mum visits, she wants to give me chicken too. And I don't even like chicken.'

'Okay. No chicken.'

'If you wouldn't mind getting me some eggs, I'll do your grandad egg and chips for tea.'

'Can we sit here a minute?' Greta heads for the bench beside the ice cream kiosk. 'I'm dying for a smoke.'

'I'm impressed you managed to wait so long.'

Greta lights a cigarette, inhaling deeply.

The sea and sky are a vibrant blue; a white speed boat bounces over the waves across the bay. 'D'you want to go for a walk before we go back? Along the sea front,' she points in the direction of The Grand Hotel.

Greta squints in the sun. 'All right.'

'Queenie and Muriel are coming round this morning for a prayer meeting, so we might as well.'

They wander along the promenade, past the boating lake, the putting green, to where the kiosks end and a narrower footpath continues alongside the open stretch of sand.

'I'm sorry my gran talks so much.'

'It's okay; she's funny. I wish we weren't going back.' The wind has blown Greta's hair into a tangled blonde mass in front of her eyes.

'I was thinking,' she says, slowly, 'why don't you talk to someone? You might… be able to get some advice.'

'Advice?' Greta stops and stares at her. 'About what?'

'I don't know… About what you went up on stage for at the celebration.'

'Who can I talk to about that?'

'Someone - like Francesca. She might know the best thing to do.'

Greta tugs her packet of Embassy No 1 from her shoulder bag. 'I don't know. I'll think about it.'

'I'll make you some sandwiches to eat on the train. There's ham in the fridge.'

They're standing in the hallway with their suitcases. 'There's no time, Gran. We had lunch in that new café, the one next to the second-hand bookshop.'

'I suppose there were people smoking in there. I've never been in a cafe in my life.'

'Never been in a cafe?' Greta repeats.

Gran thinks for a moment. 'Oh, yes we did: once, in Glasgow. Grandad and I had chips.'

'Where *is* Grandad?' Sam asks. 'I wanted to say goodbye.'

'He's just nipped out to QuikSave for a pint of milk. He'll be back in a minute.'

'We have to go, Gran, or we'll miss the train.'

'You do what you have to, dear. It's been lovely to see you.' Gran beams from Sam to Greta. 'If I go to be with the Lord, you can think to yourself that at least you've seen me one last time.'

'But you look so well, Mrs Loveday!' Greta adopts her charming smile. 'Thanks for having me. I've had a great time.'

'You're always welcome here.'

'Thanks, Gran.' She picks up her suitcase.

'Let me say a prayer for you before you go.' Gran's eyes snap tightly shut. 'Lord, I pray for these two girls now.' Her voice has changed pitch, her hands raised. 'They have chosen the path of darkness, the road to Hell. They are lost in their sinful ways…'

She glances towards Greta, whose eyes widen.

'Let them realise, Lord, that darkness will surely bring suffering and destruction to their lives. Let them see the terrible wrong that they are doing and find your saving grace. Forgive them, Lord, and show them your guiding light once more...'

'Right then. Thanks again, Gran.' She pushes Greta out of the front door.

Her grandmother follows, whispering into her ear, 'She's wicked, that one!'

Nineteen

Revelations

Not long now, she thinks, as the train pulls out of Winchester station. Greta is asleep on the seat opposite, curled up with her head resting on her yellow sweatshirt, strands of blonde hair falling across her cheek.

She lets her eyelids drift shut. 'Dear God, please give me a vision.'

Slowly, she opens them again. The train is passing an industrial estate: a grey sprawling factory with rows of chimneys. The window is misted up, she notices, coated in grime on the outside. God is showing her that her life's like the window, she realises: she's on one side, he on the other. The grime is her sin, preventing her from having a clear vision of him. He's telling her to change her attitudes and thoughts and live a life of purity and holiness, as Jesus did, and then she'll have a clean view of him. The Holy Spirit is the sun, shining in through the window, through the relationship between herself and God.

Soon she'll be back in her bedroom at home and she can write the picture in her new journal; she purchased the red hardback notebook from a gift shop in Hove, to record all her messages from God.

Her mother's green Mini is parked in one of the short stay spaces in Temple Meads car park.

'Hello girls.' Her mother kisses her cheek.

Sam lifts their suitcases into the boot.

'Did you have a nice time, Greta?'

'Yes, thanks.' Greta scrambles into the back seat.

'You've had good weather.'

'It's been sunny all week,' she says. 'We've had loads of walks by the sea.'

Her mother smiles back at Greta. 'You'll have to come again with Sam's dad and me, and we'll take you further along the coast to Rye.'

'Thanks.'

'How's Gran?'

'Okay.' Sam glances at her friend. 'She was a bit odd, though, when we were leaving.'

'What's she done?'

'It doesn't matter.' Greta had joked about it afterwards, but she's hard to work out these days. 'It was fine before that.'

'That's good. Oh, Joe phoned for you.'

'Did he?'

'He said he has to speak to you today.'

'I just wanted to explain why.' Joe's voice is subdued on the other end of the telephone line.

'It's all right. You don't need to.' She's been home for five minutes, sufficient time for her to have read his letter. She knew it was from him, as soon as she laid eyes on the long slanted handwriting on the envelope.

'I've been praying this week,' he continues. 'God's got important plans for my life.'

'Mm.'

'He reminded me that marriage is divine – it's when he chooses two people to use together for him.'

'I know.'

'Can you *listen*! This is important! I'm trying to explain there's not enough unity between us. If it was God's will for us to be together, then I'd know it, without any doubt.'

'Yes. I agree.'

'Do you?'

'I've been thinking the same thing myself.'

'You have?'

'We've not been close for ages.'

'I wouldn't say that.'

'It's true: you know it is. We don't get on anymore.'

He hesitates. 'I… think we need to talk about this.'

'Do we?'

'We'll go for lunch tomorrow in town, to that Greek-'

'I'm meeting my sister tomorrow. Anyway, what's the point, if we're finishing?' She laughs.

'D'you think it's funny?'

'No.' She stifles another nervous laugh.

The telephone line has gone dead.

The smell of fried onions wafts through the hallway.

'Tea will be half an hour,' her mother says, when she puts her head around the kitchen door. 'Chilli con carne.'

'If Joe phones, could you tell him I'm not here?'

Her mother looks across the room in surprise. 'Is everything all right, love?'

'Yeah. I just don't want to speak to him again today. Will you tell him I've gone out with Dad?'

Her mother frowns. 'Well, okay. If you want.'

Her bedroom is still and quiet, the open window letting in the cool evening air. She has stacked her school books on the floor, leaving a clear space on her desk, on which her Bible and the new red notebook are prized open. She re-reads her first journal entry: 'God is saying, use effectively for him every minute you have as life is short. (Doing schoolwork is also giving glory to God.)' Underneath, she has written a description of the window revelation.

'Dear God,' she prays, 'please speak to me again now.'

Leafing through her Bible, she slides her finger randomly across the page that falls open: 'Forgetting what lies behind and straining forward to what lies ahead, I press on towards the supreme and heavenly prize to which God in Christ Jesus is calling us upward.' That's perfect, she thinks, carefully underlining the verse and copying it into the red book.

'Sam!' her mother is calling up the stairs.

'Yeah?'

'Joe's here.'

Her heart sinks.

He's waiting in the hallway, clutching a bunch of pink roses. Her mother is talking to him, an anxious expression on her face. 'Why don't you two go out in the garden?'

She places the flowers in the kitchen sink; Joe follows her out to the patio at the back of the house. As soon as they're alone, he draws her close and kisses her. His lips are cold; he tastes like beer and cigarettes.

She pulls away, sitting on one of the garden chairs. 'You've had a cigarette.'

'Of course I haven't.' He drags a chair close to hers.

The cat has followed them outside and squats under the washing line.

'Have you had a good week?' she asks.

'What do *you* think? I've had a lot on my mind, obviously.' He sighs, heavily. 'I need to ask Kurt about it - he always understands stuff - but he's away. I tried Francesca but no-one's answering the phone.'

'She's probably away as well.'

He shakes his head. 'Kurt said she'd be at home. She's probably having difficulties again or something.'

'Difficulties?'

'Feeling down or whatever. Kurt said she sometimes doesn't want to see anyone.'

'Really? I hope she's okay. You've not seen her this week, then?'

'I just said that. Look, we need to talk.'

'What about?'

'You know what about.'

'You said in the letter you thought we should finish,' she tries to sound serious, 'and I think so too. It'll be good to have more time to revise for my exams.'

'What's that got to do with it?'

'It's not just that. We're really different.'

'How can you say that? You don't even seem *upset*.'

She can't think of a reply.

He gazes at her, mournfully. 'I always thought we'd get married. I can't imagine being with anyone else.' He tries to take her hand. 'We could still get off together sometimes.'

She scoops up the cat into her arms to carry him inside. 'Let's give it some time,' she says over her shoulder.

Twenty

Heaven and Hell

The branches of the willow tree across the street hang perfectly still. The sounds of water running and the chink of crockery drift up from the kitchen downstairs where her mother is clearing away the breakfast things.

'Stella?' her mother had exclaimed, when she'd said she was meeting her sister in Bristol this afternoon.

'We arranged it last week, remember?'

She can't remember the last time she and Stella did anything together. What if they run out of things to talk about? 'Dear God, please help me to get on well with Stella today,' she prays, quickly. 'And give me the chance to speak to her about you.'

Her Bible lies open on the desk. God is reminding her, in the New Testament, of her reason for being here in the world: to tell others about him. She has an obligation; what she says might be the only chance to stop a person going to Hell. If she truly loves Stella, she should do all she can to save her soul for eternity. It's not just her sister, she thinks, but all the other people she knows at school who don't believe. She must find the right moment to tell them the truth.

She turns to a clean white page in her journal and picks up her fountain pen. 'If Jesus comes tomorrow,' she writes, 'it will be too late and my friends will go to Hell. I have a responsibility.'

The bus trundles along the High Street, halting at the traffic lights. As she gazes through the window at the row of shops, the last building, J.H. Brown Undertakers, catches her attention. Sensing another vision forming in her mind, she closes her eyes. She has died and is sitting in Heaven, looking down upon the world with a heavy heart as she sees all the people she used to know, still blind. She's longing to be able to help them but it's too late; her years of opportunities have been wasted. God wants her to realise, she thinks, that he could come and take her at any time. Now is the time to tell everyone about him; what if Jesus comes tomorrow and her friends are sent to Hell? She says another quick prayer for Stella. She must find the courage to talk to her today.

She presses the buzzer as the bus approaches the corner of

Zetland Road, where Stella has told her to get off. The street is lined with pubs and cafes, record and jewellery shops. She's been here before, one Saturday a few months ago. Greta had wanted to look in the second-hand clothes shops. They spent hours wandering from one charity shop to the next, trying on garish shirts and dresses, hand-knitted cardigans in turquoise and bright pink wool. Sam bought a knee-length scarlet jumper and Greta had her nose pierced in the hairdressing salon.

'You won't feel anything,' the woman with dyed strawberry-blonde hair said, but afterwards the side of Greta's nose swelled into a purple lump.

'It really hurts!' Greta groaned, on the telephone, that evening. 'I'll have to take it out.'

'Let me treat you,' Stella says. 'What would you like? Coffee?'

The aroma of coffee beans wafts through the cafe. 'Okay.'

'Let's have a slice of cake each, too.' Her sister gestures towards the trays of fat, wholesome-looking cakes and pastries.

'You choose something.'

Stella carries the tray with the cappuccinos and two slices of carrot cake coated with white lemony icing to the seating area upstairs, where Bohemian types hang out around wide communal wooden benches. She chooses one of the smaller tables in the corner. 'This is nice, isn't it?'

Sam nods, scraping off some of the lemon icing from her cake with her fingertip.

'I wasn't sure if you'd like it round here.'

'I've been before, with Greta.'

'Oh, how was your visit to Brighton?'

'Okay.'

'And Gran and Grandad?'

'Gran didn't stop talking the whole time; we kept going down to the seafront to escape. She said she's expecting you to get married soon.'

Stella laughs, stirring the swirls of chocolate powder into the frothy milk at the top of her cappuccino. 'She's been saying that for years.'

'I told her it wasn't likely to be soon.'

'What did Greta think of them?'

'She sat by Gran on the settee and listened to all the stories. You know what it's like.' She scoops a piece of the spongy cake onto her fork. 'But something weird happened when we were leaving...'

Her sister looks up.

'Gran started praying for us.'

'She always does that.'

'Yeah, but then she said Greta was wicked.'

'She said that to Greta?'

'It was more to me; I don't think Greta heard. But I don't understand why she said that: they were getting on really well.'

'You know what Gran's like; it could've been anything. It could be the way Greta looks. I remember Grandad offering to give me money if I promised never to dye my hair or use make-up.'

She swallows another forkful of cake. 'Greta's got this pink streak in her hair. It won't wash out.'

Stella sips her cappuccino. 'Could be that, or maybe she smelt of cigarettes. Does she still smoke?'

She nods.

'You know what Gran's like about that,' Stella grins. 'Smoking's a vice of the Devil.'

'D'you think it was that?'

'Probably. Don't worry about it.'

'I hope Greta didn't hear. You see, I'm praying for-'

'Stop worrying. How's everything else going? How's Joe?'

'Oh, we finished.'

'Goodness, have you? When did that happen?'

'Last night. It's all right; I didn't want to go out with him anymore. He's so *boring*.'

Stella smiles. 'We should celebrate then. If you've got a bit more time, we could meet up more often.'

'That'd be great. Actually..., I was going to ask if you want to come to a barbeque on Thursday.'

'A barbeque?'

'With the youth group, in Portishead. It's in the park by the lake.'

'With that youth leader? Kurt, wasn't it?'

'Kurt and Francesca.'

'I don't think so.'

'But I'd really like you to come. I know Greta'd like to see you.'

'I don't mind arranging to see *you*, but not with the youth group.'

'But why not? You used to go.'

Stella lifts her cup to her mouth, gazing at her, steadily, over the gold-striped rim. 'A long time ago.'

'But why? Why did you stop going?'

'We'll talk about it sometime.'

'Why can't you tell me now?'

'Because I'm enjoying myself and I don't want to go into it now.'

'But I *do*. It's *important*!'

Stella shrugs and smiles

'But, I…' She drops her fork onto the plate and looks away.

Stella scrapes the last mouthful of icing from her plate. 'Fancy a look around the shops?'

Twenty-one

Precious

'Two hands are clasped around a glowing sphere,' she writes, on a fresh page in her journal. 'The space around the sphere is dark and the person is holding onto it dearly, as if it's the most precious thing in the world.'

She gazes out of the bedroom window. It feels wonderful to be the first one up in the house, the only one awake in the entire street; the houses across the road look unreal in the early morning haze. God gave her the vision of the sphere during the praise and worship time in the meeting last night. She was amazed, later in the service, when the visiting minister from the Cardiff Christian Fellowship made the interpretation clear through his sermon on the book of Timothy.

'God has given us precious things,' Pastor Jones said. 'He has given us his name and he has given us his word, to treasure and keep for him.'

'We must look after what God has given us,' she writes in her journal, 'and hold onto our vision of him'.

She places her fountain pen down on the desk, closes the red notebook and lowers her eyelids. It's frustrating that she has to rush her quiet time this morning. Christian Union is taking the second year assembly today and she has her first GCSE maths paper at nine o'clock. She can spend longer later, though; after the exam, she doesn't have to go into school again until the geography paper tomorrow.

'Dear God, I pray for the assembly this morning; use us to show your love to others in the school. And I pray that I'll do well in my exam. And Greta.'

She mustn't forget her sister, she thinks. Stella wouldn't talk to her on Saturday about whatever the problem is, but it's clear she's blocking God from her life. 'I pray for Stella, Lord. I'm not sure what I should do to help her but I know you'll give me an opportunity somehow.'

It's so exciting to see all her prayers working, like on holiday, when Greta agreed to talk to Francesca about God: that was a definite answer to prayer. 'Thank you for giving me the chance to talk to Greta in Brighton, and thank you for making her listen.'

Kurt and Francesca weren't at church yesterday, or she would have asked Francesca about it straight away. She'll see her this morning in the assembly; maybe she'll have chance then. 'Thank you for Francesca. I know she'll be able to help Greta put her life right with you. Amen.'

'Ugh!' Greta clutches her head as they wander across the school yard towards the gymnasium. 'That was so embarrassing!'
She pictures them all again, standing in a line on the stage while Mr Tippits addressed the whole of the second year in that timid, dreary voice. They had sung 'Shine Your Love', Colin Patterson playing the guitar, some of the more courageous ones raising their hands in the air. 'Did you see who was at the back of the hall?'
'I know!'
She'd felt herself grow hot, suddenly noticing Mr Allen's familiar grey-flecked shirt and cords. If only Francesca had been there! She would have been proud to stand by her any day. 'I wonder where Francesca was?'
'God knows! She organised the bloody thing.'
'Mr Tippits will put people off coming to the meetings.'
Greta groans again. 'He puts *me* off!'
There had been a similar occasion in one of the Tuesday after-school prayer meetings. Francesca left the room to fetch a board marker and Mr Tippits decided to kick off the meeting with a long prayer. Just at the most tedious point, Mr Allen opened the door to the conference room. He looked surprised to see them there, averted his eyes with a half smile, apologized for disturbing them and rushed off. She can still feel the rocks of embarrassment dropping to the bottom of her stomach.
'Better try and forget about it.' They have reached the entrance to the gym. On the other side of the glass double doors, Mr Bevan and Miss O'Keefe are setting out the maths papers on the rows of wooden desks. The entire fifth year is waiting outside; there's a nervous buzz of anticipation.
'It's cruelty to children, making us do exams in this heat,' Greta moans.
'Maybe it'll be cooler in the hall.'
'At least we're not doing P.E. That's a thought; do you realise we'll never have another P.E. lesson ever again?'

'Unless you join the sixth form hockey team.' She glances across the yard to where Michaella Stones and Danielle Smith are leaning against the railings, pink-lipsticked mouths chewing gum. Michaela is made up as though about to embark on a night out in Spirals, the nightclub in the shopping precinct, her face plastered with fierce make-up, her overgrown fringe hair-sprayed into a flick over her eyes.

She'll never forget running up and down the hockey pitch every winter when the ground was white with frost, nose and fingers turning blue, trying to safely avoid Michaella - who always played Centre Forward - thundering towards you bellowing 'slag', or ramming into you if you stood in her way. Their two P.E teachers, Mrs Bird - who looks like Cagney, in Cagney and Lacey, and Mrs Crawford - who wears sunglasses and red lipstick and can't shout loud enough to gain everyone's attention - would occasionally make an appearance at the end of the pitch, dressed in thick overcoats and gloves, to check the score, blow the whistle and instruct them to swap ends, before disappearing back into the P.E office. Poor Andrea Davis had it the worst: she can still recall the sound of Michaela's wooden stick slapping against Andrea's ankles, Andrea turning scarlet, her head stooped until her eyes stopped watering. Then, 'She's fuckin' crying again!' Shrieks of hysterical laughter. Everyone else was just glad it wasn't them.

Greta rolls her eyes towards Julia Lamb, bent anxiously over a text book. 'You done much revision?'

'A bit. Have you?'

'Course I have,' Greta grins.

'I've prayed about it,' she says.

Greta raises her eyebrows.

'And for your exam.'

'Thanks.' Greta looks faintly puzzled. 'Hey, I still can't believe you and Joe have actually finished.'

'It's not a big deal.'

'You okay about it?'

'Yes, I told you. We weren't right together.'

'He was looking at you all dewy-eyed in the service yesterday.'

'No he wasn't!'

'He was! You never notice anything.'

She glances over to the entrance where Mr Bevan is propping open the doors and asking people to line up.

'I hate this!' Greta groans. 'I can't wait to get out of this place.'

'It'll be all right once the exams have finished.'

'It won't. School will always be crap! *And* living here! I hate it! I'm going as soon as I can.'

'Going? Where?'

'I don't care! As long as it's away from here.'

Twenty-two

Outreach

Sam wishes she had put on something warmer than a t-shirt; the sun is low over the estuary and there's already a chill in the air. The smell of burgers wafts over from the barbeque under the oak tree where Kurt is supervising Joe and Robin. Francesca is standing beside the picnic table, wearing an Arran pullover today: a classical country look, Sam thinks; it suits her olive skin. Now would be a good time to ask her.

The Formica picnic table is cluttered with packets of burger buns and hot dog rolls, cardboard plates and cups, plastic bottles of Coca cola and Fanta Orange.

'Francesca?'

'Hi there! Help yourself to a bread roll and fizzy drink.'

Standing close up, she's taken aback by the change in Francesca's appearance: the skin on her face is drained of colour; her eyes are puffy and ringed with shadows.

'Did you have a good holiday?' Francesca's smile is strained.

'Yeah, we went to stay with my grandma and grandad in Brighton.'

'Brighton?'

'It's by the sea; it's not far on the train.'

'Sounds like fun.'

'Erm… I was speaking to Greta on holiday, and she could really do with talking to someone about God… I thought you'd be a good person to ask.'

'Sure.'

'I told Greta I'd mention it and find out when'd be a good time to see you. We're on study leave but we've got an English revision session tomorrow, so we can stay on for C.U.'

'There's not much time in the lunch break. How about next week? Are you coming in for the prayer meeting on Tuesday?'

'We could do.' Greta won't be happy about that, she thinks.

'We could have a chat at the end.'

'Okay,' she smiles. 'I'll tell Greta.'

Francesca nods, reassuringly.

She follows her gaze towards Greta, standing by the barbeque, laughing with Irish Adam and ensuring that her vegetarian sausages are wrapped in tin foil.

'I tried to get my sister to come tonight,' she says, on impulse.
'Did you?'
'I'm worried there's something wrong. I'm praying for her.'
'That's great.'
'I'm trying to get her along to a meeting.'
'Good. It looks like the boys have finished the hot dogs - are you coming?' Francesca heads towards the oak tree where the others are queuing.

She picks up a paper plate and tears a bread roll from the packet. She'll have to go over there and talk to Joe; it's unavoidable.

'Have you seen Francesca?' Greta whispers, joining her on the tartan picnic blanket. 'What's the matter with her?'

She shrugs. 'I don't know. Maybe she's not well. Would you ask one of the boys? I don't want to speak to Joe again.'

She watches Greta saunter over to the tree where the boys are packing up the cooking equipment. Joe's grey jumper is lying on the grass, she notices, her arms still feeling cold; in the past she would have just slipped it on without asking. She senses him looking over at her and averts her eyes to where Francesca is packing the leftover food into plastic carrier bags.

'It's a migraine.' Greta flops beside her on the rug. 'Nick seems to know. Here, stick that on.' She shoves her denim jacket into Sam's arms. 'You look freezing.'

'Thanks. We'd better go over there.' The group is moving to sit in a circle on the mish-mash of blankets and coats laid out on the grass.

'And there was this woman on the course - Christine,' Kurt is saying. 'She's something else! You all have to meet her at the festival. She's set up seminars all over the country helping people express their faith using painting and music and dance. We're gonna have to invite her over here.'

'I could set up something with dance, Kurt.' Pippa smiles, flirtatiously. 'I love dancing!'

'I can see that.' Kurt winks. 'God wants you to use your gifts!'

She watches Joe, his acoustic guitar suspended from a leather strap around his neck, beginning to lead everyone singing 'I Believe in

You'.

An elderly man walking a Golden Retriever by the lake keeps looking across the park in their direction. A group of teenage boys hanging around the benches in the children's play area are staring and laughing. She's trying not to feel inhibited, but it's not easy; she isn't used to so much exposure. Kurt said this is a form of outreach, publicly making a stand for what they believe in. What other people think of her isn't important compared to the things of God, she reminds herself.

Robin picks up his Bible and notebook, contemplatively. Everyone follows, reaching into bags and jacket pockets for their own Bibles. Robin is delivering the message this evening; Kurt's idea is that each member of the Youth Ministry Team takes a turn to give a word from God, as part of their training for greater things in the future.

Robin smiles around the group, 'I've prayed about this and I feel that God wants me to talk to you tonight about growing spiritually. I know that's an area we're all aiming for.'

Sam glances towards Joe again: he looks deep in his own private world.

'As I see it, there are three main aspects of a growing spirituality: first, and most importantly, getting your relationship right with God; secondly, staying pure, in thought and actions; thirdly, gaining more knowledge, through the Bible, church speakers, listening to God.'

Will she be giving a message to the group soon, she wonders? She could easily come up with something as good as Robin.

'If a baby doesn't grow then something is terribly wrong. We must be continually growing in our relationship and walk with God. If not, then we are spiritually deformed.'

Francesca is kneeling on a bamboo mat between Pippa and Nick; Pippa's in the way, blocking her view of Francesca's face. How easy it was to talk to her tonight, she thinks. She hadn't intended mentioning her worries about Stella, but she could say anything to Francesca and she'd understand.

Robin closes his Bible, gazing around the group intensely. 'God is sad when we lay aside his gifts. I believe he wants us to take up these tools and make full use of them now. We have our whole lives ahead of us and there are so many opportunities to serve him.'

'Thank you, Robin,' Kurt says. 'There's certainly a lot there for us to go away and think about some more.'

She tugs the sleeves of Greta's jacket down over her hands. It's growing dark. The boys have gone from the children's play area; there is just one dog walker still out, his silhouette a dot in the distance by the estuary.

'Before you go, there's something I'd like you all to pray about over the coming week.' Kurt has an urgency in his voice. 'While I was away last week, God spoke to me many times about the future of our work together. There will be time for me to tell you more in our coming meetings. To begin with, I want you to organise yourselves into small prayer groups: groups of three or four. I'd like you to meet in your groups once a week; it's up to you to work out when and where. I want you to pray together and seek three visions from God: a vision for your own lives, a vision for the youth group and a vision for the church.'

She glances towards Greta; she can talk to her on the way home. They just need to decide on one or two others to join them.

'Pray for ideas to bring together young people from all over the city, and let's look towards making this a reality this summer.'

She smiles; there are so many exciting plans spinning through her mind.

Twenty-three

A Good Witness

'This is our last revision class.' She glances sadly around the English classroom. She and Greta are sitting at their usual desk in the corner.

'Is it?'

'Don't you look at your timetable?'

'Yeah - every morning.'

'The English exam's next Monday, in three days.'

Greta nods, vaguely.

'This is our last class - ever - with Mr Allen.'

'Except you're taking English in the sixth form.'

'Yeah,' she lowers her voice, 'but Caroline White said Mr Allen's leaving.'

'Is he?'

'Shh!'

'Why didn't you tell me?'

'I only just found out, when you went to get your folder.'

'How come Caroline knows?'

She shrugs. 'She said he's going to retrain as a lawyer,' she whispers.

Greta scowls across the room towards the back of Julia Lamb's blue school jumper. 'It better not be anything to do her bloody complaining!'

Her eyes sadly follow the teacher around the room: his black, wiry hair, cut short at the back and longer on top, his pale skin that blushes easily and bright blue eyes. He's not attractive in the usual way, like Ralph Macchio or Tom Cruise. He's handing back the autobiographical essays that they were asked to write before half term: a piece entitled 'A Day in the Life of…', based on a weekly column in The Guardian magazine written by a different celebrity each week.

'Be honest about how you feel,' he'd encouraged them. 'For instance, if I was writing about myself, I'd say I wish I'd become an airline pilot - not a teacher.'

She stayed up late the night before it was due in, writing about Joe: how she'd realised they were too different to go out together; how she's scared that if she doesn't pass her GCSE's, she might end up stuck in Clevedon, doing the same boring job every day for the rest of her life.

'Dear God, please use my words to speak to Mr Allen,' she prayed, as she described waking up at six o'clock every morning to read her Bible, pray and listen to what God wants to say to her. 'I know that God is there with me,' she'd written, 'and I never have to worry about anything.'

She catches the faint odour of tobacco as Mr Allen approaches their table. She saw him smoking once, through the door to the staff room. With a sweep of his hand and a bright smile, he places their marked essays on the desktop.

'Another A!' Greta prods Sam's waist when he turns to another table.

She picks up Greta's piece of work, also with a red circled A, and read out the comment. 'This really made me laugh.'

Greta grins. 'If I fail my exams, I could become a comedian.'

'When's the Festival of Light again?' Greta has swung around ninety degrees in her chair, with her back to Colin Patterson, who has, annoyingly, once more, joined Sam and Greta in their usual spot at the far end of the conference room.

'In three weeks - after the last exam. How could you forget?'

'Hello, everyone.' Francesca stands gracefully at the front, waiting for everyone's attention. 'It's fantastic to see so many of you here.' The group can no longer fit around the tables; some of the boys have had to borrow extra chairs from the maths rooms. 'First, I'd like to thank Mr Tippits here,' she turns to smile, appreciatively, at the chemistry teacher, 'for stepping in on Monday morning. I was really sorry not to be able to be there myself. Mr Tippits tells me the assembly was fantastic.'

The chemistry teacher, unfortunately now a regular weekly supporter of the Christian Union meetings, nods in agreement. His hair is as greasy as ever, making a square frame around his face and, as usual, he is wearing white socks with black shoes.

'Thanks to all of you who took part,' Francesca continues, 'for being bold and standing up for what you believe. And thanks to those on study leave who came in especially.' She glances towards Sam. 'Today's topic is Witnessing to Friends. Can you find a partner to work with?'

Thank goodness her father hadn't been available today to lead the meeting, she thinks. Her father speaking in front of the congregation at church, where he's always been, is one thing; here in school would have been so awkward.

'That's wonderful... Now, how many ways can you think of to tell your friends about Jesus?'

'Coming to the fair later?' Greta whispers, her back still to Colin.

Twice a year, Clevedon High Street is closed to traffic and the fair takes over for the weekend. 'Is it on tonight?'

'Mum said they were setting up yesterday. You could stay over.'

Francesca picks up a fat blue marker and turns to a clean sheet on the flipchart. 'So let's hear some of your ideas…'

Does Francesca know about the fair, she wonders? Maybe she'd like to go.

'Colin?'

'Invite them to C.U.,' he says, in his painfully croaky voice that desperately needs to break.

'Or to church,' Noel Stewart adds.

'Definitely,' Francesca smiles, scribbling on the chart. 'Any other ideas?

Maria's hand is up. 'Tell them ourselves about Jesus.'

'Good. Although not always that easy, is it...? Sam?'

She feels her temperature rise rapidly. 'We can be a witness through the ways we live our lives.'

Francesca beams at her across the room. 'We can all agree, can't we - this way is the most powerful.'

Her eyes fix on the varnished grains of wood in the table.

'We have to strive to be more like Jesus,' Francesca glides on, calmly, and others will look at us and see something different: God shining in us. Let me tell you a story... One day, God asked me to tell a friend about Jesus, so I sent him a letter explaining what I believe. Later that day, he called me and said he was extremely touched by the love shown in my letter: the love of God.'

Now that the attention has shifted away from her, she lifts her head. Everyone can see the love of God shining in Francesca, she thinks.

'You all need to listen to the voice of the Spirit and allow yourselves to be guided. Shall we finish with a prayer?'

She's beginning to feel ashamed for her thoughts about the assembly on Monday: that's hardly being a good witness for God. Francesca has told her she has leadership qualities; she has chosen *her*, especially, to write the C.U newsletter; she trusts her. She mustn't let her down.

'What's this?' Greta picks up an envelope resting against the flap of her satchel.

It's obvious who it's from. 'Go on! Open it!'

Greta rips open the envelope, unfolding the A4 sheet of lined paper. She runs her eyes down the page and groans.

Sam giggles, reading Colin's letter over her shoulder. 'I've liked you since in the first year. You are the most-'

Greta moves away, covering the page; 'Stop it!'

'That's sweet!'

'No it's not.' Greta clutches her forehead and moans again.

'You're cruel! I'm not telling him for you; you'll have to do it yourself.'

She has just half an hour to spare before she must collect together her wash bag and pyjamas and leave for Greta's house. She hasn't even started her evening prayer time yet and she can't miss it: her new idea of praying each evening, as well as in the mornings, is already helping her focus more on God. The Spirit has begun giving her messages, guiding her throughout the day.

She's not bothered about going to the fair tonight, anyway, she thinks, or sleeping over at Greta's. Greta might want to drink Malibu or vodka, and she'll just be annoyed when Sam doesn't want to.

She cringes, recalling her conversation with Francesca at lunchtime. She was such an idiot.

'I don't think so, Sam,' Francesca had said, her smile polite 'But thanks for mentioning it.'

Of course she wouldn't have wanted to go. Fairgrounds are for children, not sophisticated women with more interesting things to do. It's so *obvious*!

She closes her eyes, blanking out her thoughts. 'Dear God, please speak to me now. Tell me what you want me to hear.'

God's voice speaks almost at once: 'What importance do you attach to people's opinions of you? Does this hinder your relationship with me?'

She knows this is about the school assembly. 'Father, I'm sorry,' she prays. 'Please forgive me and help me to put you first in every situation.'

Twenty-four

Groups

'Slow down!' she yells, over Belinda Carlisle's 'Heaven is a Place on Earth', blasting from the loudspeaker.

Greta laughs, belting the red dodgem car around the track again, deliberately jolting against Connor Cartwright's blue and white striped car, causing him to crash into the central barrier. They have already had a head on collision with Shannon Gardner and Leanne Jackson.

The siren wails and all the cars slow to a halt.

'Phew!' Sam staggers out of the machine. 'Remind me not to go with you again.'

'You're meant to bump other cars - that's the whole point.'

'No you're not! You're meant to dodge out of people's way, not drive into them!'

'Did you see Leanne Jackson's face?'

'I didn't look.'

'Want a coke?' Greta asks, joining the queue for the burger van.

'Okay.'

'That skirt suits you.'

'You think so?'

Greta made her change out of her old jeans before they came out. 'Try this on.' She'd held up the denim mini skirt. 'Recognise it?'

'No.'

'It came from that denim pinafore I bought from the Barnados shop in Gloucester Road.'

'Crikey, that's amazing!'

'Keep it if you want - I've got too many clothes.'

Greta is wearing an outfit she's never seen before: a pair of faded cut-off jeans and a fine white cotton blouse, jangling with beads. 'You said you can never have too many clothes! Don't turn around: Jack O'Connor's over there by the rifle range. I don't think he's seen you.'

Greta glances over her shoulder. 'It's okay. He's with that second year girl.'

She turns to look again, recognising the blonde girl from school.

'Aren't they sweet together?' Greta rolls her eyes. 'He's just won her a goldfish.'

Jack is giving a bulging see-through plastic bag to the girl.

Greta pays for the drinks, passing her a can of Diet Coke.

'Thanks. Have you seen Danielle Smith?' She nods in the direction of the Octopus, its metal legs flailing in and out, the kids strapped into the seats screaming and shrieking. Behind the ticket kiosk, Danielle, in a strappy top and the shortest skirt Sam has ever seen, is practically on top of the boy operating the ride.

Greta screws up her face. 'Yuk! Let's see who can spot the most good-looking boy here.'

'I'm not in the mood.'

'It's just a game! There's no real men here, anyway.'

'Like Adam, you mean. Isn't he a bit old for you?'

'Love has nothing to do with age.'

'You hardly know him.'

'How do *you* know?'

'I thought you said he's not allowed to go out with anyone.'

'He can in seven months. I can wait.'

It's growing dark; the clash of music from the different rides seems louder and more distorted, the fluorescent lights more blinding. 'Can we leave soon?'

'Let's just drink these and have one more walk round.'

They wander past the merry-go-round, the candy-floss stall, the arcade.

'There's Sarah and Maria,' Greta shouts, over the electronic whirrs and explosions.

Her eyes scan the big wheel to where Greta is pointing; Sarah and Maria are perched in the seat right at the top, waving down at them. 'We could we ask them about the group.'

Last night, when they discussed Kurt's prayer cell idea, Greta suggested they went with Sarah McIvor and Maria Davies. 'We see them practically every day at school.'

'Will *you* ask them?' Greta says, as the girls approach the ground.

'The seat started rocking at the top,' Sarah giggles. 'We almost tipped out.'

'No, we didn't,' Maria says, sensibly.

'Are you two coming on the waltzers?' Greta asks.

They jump into a yellow and gold barrel, just in time for the Madonna track and the next ride. A red-haired boy with a leather purse strapped around his waist collects their fifty pences, winks at Greta, sets their seat spinning, and they're off, twirling so fast that the street, her friends' laughing faces, are all a blur.

She wakes with a jolt to the sound of ringing, resonating up the stairway from the hall. She lifts her wrist, trying to make out the time on her watch, but the room is pitch black.

Sitting up in her sleeping bag, she leans towards the bed. 'Greta! Wake up!'

'What?' Greta replies, sleepily.

'That was the doorbell.'

'Probably some drunk person on the way home from the pub.'

'Shouldn't we go and see?'

Greta groans. 'Go back to sleep.'

'But what if it's an emergency or something?'

There's no reply. Surely Greta hasn't gone back to sleep. How could she?

She lies down on her back and closes her eyes, keeping absolutely still. There's a creak from somewhere at the back of the house; a car drives past outside. Marine Road is away from the pubs in the High Street, she thinks. She's stayed here loads of times at weekends and it's usually quiet. Who could that have been at the door?

She gropes her way in the darkness along the edge of the bed towards the door, trying not the think about the spiders that lurk in Greta's attic bedroom: enormous, jumping ones, with thick black legs. Once on the landing, her fingers search for the light switch. The lightbulb dangling from the ceiling pings into life and she glances at her watch: almost half past one. Her hands are shaking, her heart beating quickly. What time will Lou be back? How could Greta sleep alone here in this house, with its noises, its doors and windows that won't close properly?

She creeps quietly down the creaky wooden stairs; at the bottom, she pushes another switch and the living room floods with light. She crosses the Persian rug to the window, tugs back the curtain a little and peers out: the footpath leading to the front door and the pavement beyond are deserted; the cars parked along the street are tinged orange from the street lights.

There's a sudden crash below and she catches her breath, lowering herself onto the leather settee. 'Dear God,' she prays, silently, 'please make it be okay.'

Another bang and a scuttling sound. Then she remembers the kittens in the basement. Leaving the hallway light on, she slips back up the stairs to the attic and sinks inside the comfort of her sleeping bag.

Twenty-five

Messages

'Come on then! Your top three boys you'd like to spend an evening with? You still haven't said yours.'

Greta takes a bite from her slice of toast, chewing thoughtfully.

They are sitting at the breakfast table in the alcove by the bay window. The kitchen is overrun with cats: one of the kittens scrambling in Greta's boots, the other two wrestling in a heap on the table top; the elder cat sprawled out in the sun trap on the window ledge.

'I can already guess,' Sam states.

'Okay, number one - Adam, two - Mr Allen, and three... It's difficult!'

'You have to choose someone.'

'I don't know... Ben from church, then.'

'Really?'

'But only if he wasn't going out with Avril.'

'None of your list are available!'

'I told you, Adam will be, next January.'

She nods, dubiously. Her thoughts are interrupted by the doorbell.

'They'll wake Mum!' Greta dashes to answer. 'I told Maria to *knock*.'

'We could meet here once a week,' she suggests, 'if that's all right, Greta?'

They are seated on the array of brightly coloured floor cushions in Greta's bedroom.

'Fine with me.'

'Hadn't you better ask your mum first?' Maria chips in.

Maria smells of bread, she notices; she's come straight from her early morning Saturday job at Gregg's. She glances at her short mousy hair, National Health glasses, brown shirt buttoned up to the collar, blue drainpipe jeans and white trainers; she knows what Greta will be thinking: Maria could do with a serious make-over.

'Mum's okay about people coming round,' Greta replies, 'She's never up on Saturday mornings.'

'Your house is enormous,' Sarah says, 'for just you and your mum...'

Sarah's hair is purple today, and she has on green leggings, an oversized t-shirt with a square of pink floral material stitched on the front, an assortment of different shaped and coloured rings and bracelets clinking from her wrists to her elbows.

'I mean, you're lucky,' Sarah smiles. 'It's so big! There must be loads of empty rooms.'

'Not really. You get used to spreading out.'

Sarah sits forward. 'Shall we go round and say the things we want to pray about?'

'I want to pray about my brother,' Maria says.

Maria's brother, Richard, is in their year at school and hangs out with Michaela Stones and Danielle Smith, smoking outside the school gates at lunchtime.

Maria frowns. 'I'm worried about him drinking.'

'And we can pray about Scott, my ex-boyfriend,' Sarah sighs. 'He's depressed.'

She remembers Greta telling her about Scott calling at her house that time.

'The doctor's given him tablets and Scott says it's my fault for finishing with him.'

'That's unfair,' Sam says. She's already decided what her request will be: 'I'd like us to pray for my sister, Stella. She stopped coming to church a long time ago; I don't know why. I think there's some problem.'

The others nod, seriously.

'What about you?' She glances towards Greta, leaning against the wall on a red floor cushion.

'My mum and dad.' Greta twists a section of blonde hair around her forefinger. 'And Grandma and Grandad.'

Everyone knows about the trouble between Greta's parents, and that Lou has never even set foot in a church, and Greta's grandparents are the sort of people who think they're Christians because they go to the Church of England on Christmas Eve and Easter Sunday, but they aren't really saved: they won't go to heaven.

They close their eyes, Sam hoping that the two spiders, each as big as her hand, clinging to the beams above, will stay put until they've finished.

'Heavenly Father,' Maria begins, 'I'd like to pray for those we love today. Firstly, Richard: please help him not to be led astray by others. Look after him, Lord, and I pray that one day he'll come to find you. Amen.'

'Dear God, I pray for Stella…' Her words seem to fall into a strange empty space; a muffled giggle erupts from Greta's side of the room. She opens her eyelids to see Maria frowning, and turns her head so that Sarah is blocking the line of vision between Greta and herself. 'I ask that I'll find a way of talking to her about you. Amen.'

'Lord,' Sarah prays, 'I bring Greta's family to you today - show them your love. And I pray for Scott – help me to know the right thing to do. Amen.'

'Please speak to each of us,' Maria asks, 'and tell us what we should do about the things in our lives that are troubling us. Amen.'

They wait, silently. She stares at the dark insides of her eyelids.

'I have a picture of a car driving around a roundabout,' Sarah says, suddenly. 'That's like my relationship with Scott and God is saying, it's simple: I just need to turn off in a different direction and drive away.'

Everyone nods, lowering their heads again.

'And I can see a rope,' Sarah continues. 'That's for you, Sam, to give to Stella to help save her. You have to encourage and support her, and she'll make a commitment to God.'

'I think I might have a picture,' Greta says, unexpectedly. 'There's a table spread with plates of exotic food and goblets of wine.

'Do you know what it means?' Sarah asks.

'I'm not sure.'

They all close their eyes and wait for someone to receive the interpretation.

'I know,' Maria says. 'God's telling you these are his riches to give to your family.'

Sam notes down a brief description of each picture in one of Greta's old school exercise books. 'Greta, why don't you find a verse?' She picks up Maria's Good News Bible. 'Just open it anywhere and choose a line.'

Greta flips open the rainbow cover and reads, 'God is greater than our hearts and he knows everything.'

'Mm,' Sarah murmurs. 'That's why we're meeting. Write that in the book, Sam. We have to see things from God's point of view and everything makes sense.'

Greta steps over the cushions to open the skylight; the sky outside has grown dark, the air humid. Hopefully Sarah and Maria will go soon, she thinks; she wants to talk to Greta on their own before she goes to the hairdressers.

Twenty-six

Religious

The receptionist takes Sam's stonewash denim jacket and motions for her to sit on the olive leather settee by the open French windows. 'Matt won't be long. Can I get you tea or coffee?'

'No thanks.'

The girl begins sweeping the sea of blonde hair from the floor around where Matt is cutting a young woman's hair. She catches her reflection in the mirror opposite; her hair looks flat and heavy. She tries to imagine it tumbling lightly over her shoulders, like Francesca's hair. She needs a change, but nothing too drastic. She's never forgotten that time - her twelfth birthday - when she'd had her waist-length locks chopped off for a short cut and perm. That was here in Reflections, with Wendy, who she's never had since, thankfully. It's taken her this long to grow out the curls and restore her hair to its former safe length.

She meets Matt's eyes in the mirror and he smiles. His eyes are an unusual shade of green - she'd noticed that last time - contrasting his dark complexion. How old is he? Eighteen perhaps?

'So, what would you like?'

'Not too much off. The same length as before, but maybe with some layers.'

Matt runs his fingers through her hair, lifting strands from each side, assessing their lengths. 'I'll see what I can do.'

She rests her head back against the sink, closing her eyes as the warm water runs through her hair. The radio is playing Tiffany, 'I Think We're Alone Now'.

'You going out anywhere tonight?' Matt asks.

'No.' Her eyes are still closed. The sweet scent of shampoo envelopes her as he rubs the lather through her hair. 'I'm in the middle of my GCSE's.'

'I remember all that. How's it going?'

'Okay, I think.'

A wine-coloured towel is wrapped around her head like an enormous bandage and she's guided over to the black swivel chair in front of the mirror. The light in the room, reflected in the mirror, is startlingly bright. Her illuminated face, framed with wet bedraggled hair, stares back at her. She averts her eyes.

'Can you sit more to the left? That's right.' Matt begins snipping the back. 'What've you been up to, then, apart from exams?'

'Not much. I'm quite tired.'

'Late night last night?'

'I was just staying at my friend's house. Someone rang the doorbell in the night and I couldn't get back to sleep.'

Matt smiles, sympathetically. 'You look like you could do with cheering up.'

Her eyes focus on the dark mass of hair - *her* hair - falling into a heap on the white tiled floor. 'Do I?'

'Can I get you a drink after work?'

'Today?'

'Why not? You're my last cut this afternoon.'

'Oh..., okay then.'

It's almost four thirty by the time she leaves the precinct with Matt. The sky is growing darker by the minute; the air is cool on her skin.

'Your hair looks good,' Matt smiles.

'Thanks.'

'I borrowed this from Jessica in the salon, just in case.' He waves the golfing umbrella in his hand, glancing upwards. 'I thought you might like to go to The Swan. It's not far.'

He's wearing a tatty leather jacket, hanging loosely over his pale blue shirt. What would Greta say if she could see her now?

They stroll along the pathway past the sports centre, the doctor's surgery, turning into St Andrew's Walk. As the rain begins to fall fast, Matt holds the wide umbrella over them like a canopy. 'It's just over there.'

At the bar, he orders a pint of beer for himself, a coke for her, and leads her to one of the leather sofas in the back room. She slips off her damp jacket and tries to look relaxed.

'You sure I'm not stopping you from meeting your boyfriend or anything?'

'I... don't have a boyfriend.'

'I thought you might... The last time you came into the shop, you mentioned...'

'Joe? I *was* going out with him, but we broke up.'

'I'm not either... Seeing anyone, I mean.' He's drinking his pint of beer quickly. 'Me and Lucy - my ex - we finished about a month ago.'

Matt's eyes change colour in different lights, she notices; here, in the dimly-lit bar, they look almost grey.

'In the end, neither of us could be bothered. It was like that for ages: both kind of waiting for one of us to end it.'

'That's er, really sad. Had you been going out together long?' She wants to go now, back home to her familiar house, her warm bedroom...

Outside the pub, Matt steps closer.

'See you then.' She turns to leave.

'Let me walk you with the umbrella - or you'll get soaked.'

'I'm all right, honestly.'

He touches her arm as she tries to move away again. They are alone under the trees, the rain beating fast onto the umbrella that Matt is now holding over them. He lowers his head to kiss her.

'Don't,' she says quietly, pulling away.

'Why not? I thought...'

'I'm sorry.'

'What's the matter?'

'I can't... It's my religion.'

He hesitates for a moment and then smiles. 'Oh, I get it. You're religious, and I'm not. Is that it?'

'Sort of. I have to go.'

'Only if you take the umbrella - or your hair'll get messed up.'

'I don't mind the rain.' She walks away, back in the direction of the precinct. The smell of spices wafts from the Indian restaurant across the street.

'At least think about it, Sam,' he calls after her. 'It could be romantic. Like Romeo and Juliet!'

She glances over her shoulder to see him grinning; to her relief, he doesn't follow.

There are too many people on the bus. She sits in a seat by the aisle; it's only one stop to the end of Trenchard Street. She needs to take off her wet things.

'You're soaking!' Her mother helps her to unpeel her soggy jacket. 'Where've you been?'

'Greta's, and the hairdresser's. I told you.'

'You're very late!'

'I'm going to have a bath.' She heads for the stairs.

'Is anything the matter, love?' her mother calls after her.

She leans over the banister. 'Of course not. Everything's fine.'

She twists the bath taps, pouring creamy liquid from the bottle on the window ledge into the swirling water. She can't wait to speak to Greta and tell her what's just happened.

Twenty-seven

Changed

'Osmosis,' Sam reads, 'is the diffusion of water through a semi-permeable membrane.'

The roar of a motorbike engine interrupts her concentration; she turns to glimpse the flash of metal and Joe's red biker jacket through the window in the dining room, where the table is littered with hefty science textbooks and biology notes contained in faded green exercise books. Henry, dozing on a pad of paper, twitches his ears.

'Mum, it's Joe again! I'm not here, okay?' She darts upstairs before she's spotted.

In her room, she perches on the edge of the bed and waits. She's sure Joe enjoys turning up unexpectedly, accelerating along Trenchard Street on his new bike, turning the neighbours' heads. It's annoying because, after he's driven all the way to Clevedon, she feels as though she ought to talk to him, and she's not interested in hearing about his new job selling insurance, or his motorbike, or Kurt.

At church, members of the congregation have noticed that she and Joe have stopped sitting together. Mavis Day came to find her after the service on Sunday morning. She'd never spoken to Sam before but everyone knows Mavis: she dances in the aisles and frequently prophesises in tongues in the meetings; she goes forward for prayer every time there's an appeal, shrieking and collapsing when the leaders pray for her. Once, she was knocked out cold and four of the elders had to carry her out of the service. Sam thought she was dead.

Mavis put her floral-clad arm stiffly around Sam's shoulder, pulling her close. 'Now dear, God has given me a message for you.'

She tried to smile and look comfortable.

Mavis's voice lowered intimately. 'God has a purpose for your life. He wants you to know he has someone very special for you.' The grip on her arm tightened. 'Just you wait and see.'

Her mother opens her bedroom door, frowning. 'He's gone. He brought you flowers - when I said you weren't in, he threw them on the path and stamped on them. Just wait till I tell your dad!'

She groans. 'I need to make sure I get some revision done tonight; I've got two exams tomorrow. Joe doesn't understand.'

'I know, love. He shouldn't be pressuring you like this.'

She's been looking forward to this all evening: the moment when she can put away her work, think about the day and talk to God.

Her disappointment is still with her from earlier, when Mr Tippets arrived to take the after-school prayer meeting. 'I'm afraid Francesca telephoned this morning to say she's ill.'

If Sam had known that beforehand, she wouldn't have bothered to go into school to listen to boring old Mr Tippets droning on. Although, she shouldn't think like that.

'She's very sorry but she won't be able to make it today, and probably not to the Christian Union meeting on Friday either.' Mr Tippets had turned to address Greta. 'She asked me to pass on a message to you about a special meeting the two of you had planned for today.'

All eyes fell on Greta with new interest.

'She asked if you could rearrange it for the same time next week.'

Greta nodded, her face reddening.

She hopes there's nothing seriously wrong with Francesca. 'Dear God,' she prays, quickly, 'please make Francesca well again, very soon - well enough to come to Christian Union on Friday.'

Her sister comes into her mind; Stella is away in Paris this week. She mustn't despair, she tells herself, if things take time. 'Lord, please give me another opportunity to help Stella find you as soon as she's back home. Amen.'

She turns to a new chapter in her Bible study guide: Trust. 'We should never be worried or anxious,' she reads. 'God will meet all our needs if we trust him. We must have faith. God loves us and will always be there for us. Complete trust in him is so simple and yet so powerful. We need to rely on him and allow him to carry us with his spirit of peace…'

She draws the curtains, blocking out the dark street; outside, the rain batters against the window pane. She climbs into bed and wraps the duvet around her like a cocoon. From the living room below, the familiar tune signals the end of the Ten O'clock News.

What's her sister doing now in Paris? Is she out in a bar somewhere, or tucked up in a hotel bedroom? Is she alone? Sam doubts that. Maybe she's with the man from the note in her address book. She pictures her in a French restaurant, drinking wine at a candle-lit table with a dark, attractive man. Yawning, she reaches to switch on the bedside lamp and opens her journal, running bleary eyes over the indecipherable fuzz of words that she wrote earlier.

There's a light tap on the bedroom door, then her mother's voice. 'It's Emily on the phone for you.'

'Emily?' What on earth can Joe's sister want? She heard the phone ring and assumed it must be one of her aunties, calling at this time of night. 'Just a second. I'll pick up the phone in the office.'

'Where *were* you tonight?' Joe's harsh voice startles her.

'What d'you mean? And I thought it was Emily.'

He ignores her. 'I drove all the way over from Bristol and you weren't there! Your mum wouldn't even tell me where you were!'

She glances at the carriage clock on the bookshelf: it's quarter to eleven. He's phoned her at this hour, got Emily to lie for him, just to have a go at her. 'It's got nothing to do with you!'

'So where *were* you?' Joe is seething.

She doesn't have to say anything, she thinks; she's done nothing wrong. She can hear her father locking the front door for the night, treading quietly up the stairs; he passes the door carrying his night-time glass of orange juice. Her mother is turning off the lights downstairs. The office is adjacent to her parents' bedroom; soon they'll be able to hear everything she says.

'Well?' Joe demands. 'Are you going to explain?'

She picks at the corner of her father's writing pad. 'I was revising with a friend. It's nothing to make a big deal about.'

'With Greta?'

'Yes.'

'Why didn't you say so straight away?'

'You're not very easy to talk to like this.'

The telephone line is quiet. 'I'm sorry, Sam.'

She doesn't reply.

'It just seemed like you didn't care, that's all.'

She wonders if he is genuinely upset. 'I don't have to tell you everything.'

'Okay, but you do care, don't you?'

'Yes,' she says, quietly.

'Things haven't changed, have they?'

'No,' she lies, relieved that he's safely on the other side of Bristol.

Twenty-eight

Flesh and blood

'We don't have to do everything today.' Greta is lying, lazily, on her stomach, propping herself up with her elbows. 'Sarah only came up with the idea *yesterday*, and it's not happening till August. That's months away!'

'But it's not months!' Maria snaps, sounding like Mrs Comrie, their officious geography teacher. 'All three of you are going off to Southaven for the Festival of Light in a fortnight. That'll take out two whole weekends. '

'You're invited to come to the festival too, Maria.' Sarah smiles, good-naturedly.

'I told you: I can't get the time off at Greggs. The date we've decided to hold the rally on is two weeks after you get back; that only leaves us with one weekend either side of your holiday to sort things out. The whole thing is our idea so we have to make it work.' Maria scrutinises Greta for signs of comprehension.

Greta shrugs, listlessly.

'Okay, Sarah, you're responsible for the music. Sam, you're going to try and organise a drama piece, aren't you?'

'Some of the Christian Union lot might be up for it.' She can ask Emma Miles at church for a drama script.

'I'll say the opening prayer and talk about the vision,' Maria announces.

'And I'll say the final prayer.' Sarah glances at Greta. 'That just leaves someone to give a Bible message.'

Greta laughs. 'Don't look at me! Do I look like the sermon-giving type?'

'Can't we decide on that next week?' Sam nudges Greta with her foot. 'That still gives us plenty of time.'

Greta nods, looking non-committal. She's been acting strangely all morning, even when it was just the two of them before the others arrived.

'Do you think we ought to tell Kurt?' Sarah asks, anxiously.

'This is our own thing in Clevedon,' Maria states, 'just for local-'

'I think we should talk to Francesca about it,' Sam interrupts, 'if we're involving Christian Union.'

'Well, all right,' Maria concedes, 'but let's get it all organised first - show her we can do it ourselves.'

'Come on, then,' Sarah smiles. 'Let's make a start.'

They lower their heads, close their eyes.

'Dear Lord,' Sarah prays. 'Thank you for giving us the inspiration to organise our own youth rally. I commit our plans to you now. Please speak to us and give us your guidance. Amen.'

The faint ticking of Greta's plastic alarm clock on the window ledge intrudes into the silence. She's never noticed it before. She stares at the dark insides of her eyelids, trying to clear a space in her thoughts. She has had messages from God, hasn't she, when she's prayed on her own at home? But nothing seems to come when she's here. The others must think God doesn't speak to her.

'I had two pictures,' Maria begins, solemnly. 'There was an image of a churchyard full of gravestones, and another of a shining sword. God is saying that these are the graves of people we know who'll go to Hell if we don't tell them about him. And the sword is to conquer the lack of faith around us.'

Sam reaches for the group notebook next to the battered-looking box set of Enid Blyton's Chalet School books on the bookcase. Greta never throws anything away; her old toy box is still sitting there under the beams. She carefully writes the date and describes Maria's picture and its interpretation.

'I can see a desert island,' Sarah says, her eyes still closed, 'and the tide is coming in. The four of us are living on the island and we know important things. People will travel to see us to find out what we have to tell them about God.'

'Can I write, Sam?' Maria takes the notepad and pen, holding the pen poised by the open page. 'Anyone have anything else?'

'Er, I had a picture of an empty gift box.' Greta rubs her forehead with the palm of her hand. 'But I don't know what it means.'

'God is telling us we mustn't be aiming to receive anything for ourselves.' Maria scribbles as she speaks. 'What we're doing is for him.'

'Why don't you find a verse, Sam?' Sarah passes her Maria's Good News Bible.

She opens the rainbow cover and flicks through the pages, letting the book fall open. 'For our struggle is not against flesh and blood but against the powers of this dark world and against the spiritual forces of evil in the heavenly realms.'

'That's *so* relevant!' Maria looks at each of them, her pale face serious. 'If we're going to do God's work, the Devil will send enemies to fight against us.'

'That's what I've been reading about in my scripture notes!' Sarah says. 'The disciples were told not to preach anymore but they still performed miracles. All the people believed so strongly in their power, they crowded the streets to be healed.'

'What a great idea for the message at the youth rally!' Maria addresses Sam as though she's already agreed to it.

'Yeah... Possibly...' She glances towards Greta again: she's miles away.

'I think we all need to do something to show our commitment,' Maria asserts. 'We should make a sacrifice.'

'We could give up watching television,' Sam suggests. 'Most of the stuff on's boring, anyway.'

'Hang on a minute!' Greta casts her an irritated glance across the room. 'I can't give up watching Eastenders and Coronation Street.'

'It'd be hard for me to give up the TV,' Maria frowns. 'Rich always has it on in the living room.'

'I know!' Sarah says, triumphantly. 'What about giving up Neighbours? We can all manage that, can't we?'

'You sure you don't want to come into Bristol?' Sam asks. 'We could have a look in Uncle Jack's. You said you wanted to get a shirt for summer.'

Greta is huddled on one of the pillar-box red floor cushions, hugging her knees. 'Sorry.'

'What about that film - Back to the Future? It's on in Whiteladies Road.'

'Why don't you ask Sarah?'

'Don't be stupid. Go on! Let's do something! I can't relax at home if I'm not revising. How about a bike ride?'

'It's raining.' Greta glances miserably up at the grey clouds through the skylight.

'Oh, all right!' she sighs.

Greta lowers her eyelids, turning her head away.

Sam picks up her bag. 'I might call you later.'

She hurries along the promenade; her clothes are already soaked. She forgot to bring her umbrella again; it was fine this morning. There's just one other brave soul out: a figure in a blue cagoule down on the beach throwing a Frisbee for a bedraggled sheepdog; the rain has caused all the summer day-trippers to take refuge in the cafés by the amusement park. Opposite the pier, she takes the short cut through the shopping precinct: at least it's covered. She'll slip into Tesco's for some chocolate, see if the rain eases off.

Wandering down the readymade meals aisle, her eyes glaze over at the rows of plastic-packaged foods, the dazzling strip lighting. This was a mistake, she realises, trying to manoeuvre out of the way of trolleys and whining children. In the frozen food aisle, a toddler is screeching, its mother patiently trying to coax it to shut up. The woman has a smaller child draped over her shoulder, dribbling a long trail of spit down the back of her cardigan. She heads quickly past the freezers of pizzas, oven chips, Bird's Eye fishfingers. Reaching the chocolate section, she picks up a Cadbury's Flake, a treat for when she's revising. Beside the checkout, boxes of special offer red wine have been painted with the French flag, and she thinks of Stella again, flying back from Paris today.

She joins the end of a queue of women trying to supervise children and babies and, at the same time, stack boxes of Coco Pops, jumbo sacks of crisps, packets of Super-Saver Nappies, onto the conveyer belt. She should have gone into the newsagents, she thinks, staring at the red-pinnied girl behind the checkout, who looks about twelve years old. Their queue is being held up while she rings for assistance with the jammed receipt machine. The baby in the child seat of the trolley in front starts to grizzle.

She pictures Greta again, all hunched and weird-looking on the red beanbag. Suddenly, she goes cold. Something is wrong: she's sure of it. She has to go back. Without hesitation, she leaves the glossy yellow chocolate packet beside the checkout and walks to the far side of the supermarket and through the exit.

She lets herself in through the backdoor in the basement. The house is quiet; the kittens are skittering about on the floorboards in the hallway above. Lou must be in bed still; she mustn't wake her. Greta said her gig was in Taunton last night. She treads quickly up the flights of stairs to the top of the house.

Greta doesn't notice Sam standing in the doorway. She's sitting on the floor, her shirt unbuttoned, a navy blue towel draped across her lap. Scattered across the floorboards are various packages, tubes, a roll of kitchen paper.

The red of the blood is a shock, causing Sam to stand transfixed, clasping the edge of the doorway.

Greta's hand sweeps the razor over her stomach, slowly, carefully, cutting a vertical slit until it bleeds. Without pausing, she makes another cut, and another, before she lifts her head. When she catches sight of Sam, her eyes look as though they can't focus; her mouth curls into a strange kind of grimace.

Sam can't stop staring.

Greta leans back against the bed, breathes out heavily. 'You shouldn't have come in without knocking.' She calmly tears off a sheet of kitchen roll, holds it against her stomach.

Sam watches as the bright red blood is rapidly absorbed into the white paper; Greta pressing another layer over the top. 'You okay?' she asks, stupidly.

Greta slips the razor into a slim plastic box, picks up the tube of antiseptic cream. 'You're soaked, you idiot! You'd better borrow some clothes.'

Twenty-nine

Mountains

The musicians are practising before the service; the rhythm of the drums and Joe's bass guitar reverberate along St Nicholas Street. Her father strides ahead, smart in his best Marks & Spencer's grey suit and tie. Her mother is lagging behind with Jean Hutton, who's come in their car. The museum building, with its elaborate architecture and striking stained glass windows, looms impressively over Castle Park and the surrounding streets. It's the perfect place to attract converts, she thinks; far better than that dismal school in Fishponds where they used to meet. No-one new would ever have found it for a start, and the meeting hall was in the school gym, with the distinct whiff of sweaty plimsolls.

'You go on,' Greta says, as they approach the glass porch. 'I'll catch you up.'

'I don't mind waiting.' There's no sign of Irish Adam; the rehab minibus hasn't arrived yet.

'No, it's all right. I'll see you inside.'

In the foyer, Tim Goodman, beaming as usual, shakes her hand heartily. 'Good evening, young lady. And how are you?'

'Fine,' she smiles.

On the other side of the glass partition separating the foyer from the main hall, the rows of chairs are deserted; no-one is here yet except for the musicians on the platform. She moves away quickly before Joe spots her; she can't enter the hall by herself. She glances back towards the entrance: her mother and Jean Hutton are talking to Tim; her father must have gone down to the crypt. She heads for the narrow staircase leading to the balcony; there's no harm in sitting up there for a change.

She chooses a seat at the front, overlooking the rows of empty chairs below, ensuring that the line of vision between her seat and Joe's is obscured by a pillar. Of course Greta wants to talk to Adam on her own. That's what happens when you like someone. Greta had thought she was mad to walk out on Matt last week.

'Is he good looking?' Greta had interrogated her.

'Very.'

'How old?'

'About nineteen.'
'And you like him?'
'He's nice to talk to. He listens - not like Joe.'
'So I don't get it. What's the problem?'
'I don't know. It just didn't feel right!'
'I don't believe you sometimes!'

'God is not complicated.' Pastor Loveday gazes across the congregation. 'He speaks very simply to us. All we have to do is allow ourselves to *move* with him. This costs everything.'

Even the balcony is full tonight; the ushers have had to set out extra chairs in the wings. All eyes are fixed, solemnly, on the platform: the reassuring figure of her father, who looks tiny from up here.

'It's so easy to drift away from the things of God, to give in to the flesh. The desires of the flesh are naturally stronger than our spiritual desires, and so if our walk becomes weak, then we become vulnerable to this world and sin can easily creep in.'

All the way into Bristol tonight, she'd been aware of Greta's close proximity in the back of the car, her white skin beneath the fabric of her navy blue t-shirt. She's gone over and over it. And what about the odd feeling in the supermarket? Was that a sign from God?

'God has given us his gift of prayer,' her father's lilting voice continues, 'so that we can overcome all difficulties and harm that might befall us. Our prayers can move mountains, raise people from the dead; prayers can make the impossible possible.'

But *her* prayers aren't working, she thinks. She's been praying about Greta for months, and now this! And what about her prayers for Stella? She's not heard a word from her sister since they went to that cafe in Gloucester Road.

Last night, after she arrived home from Greta's, she looked up the section in her Bible study guide on prayer. There are five things that need to be right, it said, before prayers are successful: humbleness, whole-heartedness, faith, righteousness and obedience. Is she doubting too much? Not really believing? Or maybe she's not pure enough: she still has thoughts she knows are selfish. Is she stopping God from working in her life? Perhaps she's not truly filled with the Spirit at all; perhaps she's a fake. How can God fill her with the Spirit when so many things are still not right in her life?

She'll try harder, she resolves. She must put her relationship right with God.

Her eyes move across the hall below, to the end of the second row where Francesca is sitting; she's wearing that deep blue dress with the ruffled sleeves. She can't see her face properly but it's such a relief that she's well again. It'll be all right, she thinks; Francesca will speak to Greta soon and she'll know what to do. Francesca is the only one she can trust and rely on.

Everyone in the auditorium stands. She watches her father lead the singing; Joe, on the left of the stage next to Lucy Longthorn, holding his white guitar like a rock star; Clive Winstanley playing the drums; Megan Morris in her usual seat at the keyboard. She scans the rows behind Francesca: she still can't see Greta or Adam. Unless they came in late, she thinks, turning to glance across the balcony.

Her eyes at once meet a familiar gaze: Stella! She's locked to the spot, stunned, as light floods over her sister.

The music is beginning to slow; in a few seconds, everyone will be seated. But before she can think, her sister has disappeared through the archway leading to the staircase. She follows, darting down the stone stairway, through the foyer and out into the bright daylight of St Nicholas Street. Stella has vanished.

Back in the hall, her father has asked the congregation to close their eyes for a time of open prayer. She shuts out the quiet murmuring, the soft singing, and slips into her own thoughts. She tries to recall Stella's face, her expression just now when their eyes had met, but the memory is blurred. What can she do? She needs to talk to her. Stella came here! Her prayer was answered.

Thirty

Guidance

Sam glances towards Francesca, who is moving swiftly around the conference room, stooping to pick up crumpled scraps of paper, abandoned biros with chewed plastic ends. Greta is glued to her seat by the window, even though the rest of the circle of chairs has been cleared away. She ignored Sarah's and Maria's curious glances, their calls goodbye, instead fiddling with something intently in her bag while most of the group, one by one, drifted off home.

'I'll bring my guitar on Friday.' Noel beams at Francesca. He and Colin Patterson always hover behind after the meetings.

Francesca straightens the notes on her clipboard, closes the zip on her leather handbag. 'That's great, Noel.'

'What songs do you want?'

'You decide. You know what'll go down well.'

Noel turns crimson. 'Thanks.'

Colin's eyes keep darting across the room towards Greta. If she's noticed, she isn't showing it.

Francesca places a hand on each of the boys' shoulders, steering them towards the door. 'See you on Friday.'

'Okay, Francesca. See you Friday.'

As they saunter off, Colin sneaks another glance over his shoulder towards her friend.

'So...' Francesca drags a chair over beside them.

Greta is still holding her satchel on her lap.

'Sam said you could do with talking.' Francesca's tone is soothing. 'I've been worried about you.'

The school bell rings, signalling the end of after-school detention.

'I have to go,' Sam says, quickly. Her sister phoned last night: 'Let's have tea in The Balmoral. I could meet you straight from school.'

Greta nods, avoiding her eyes.

'Are you sure you can't stay?' Francesca asks, calmly.

'I'd like to, but my sister's waiting for me.' Sam slings her bag over her shoulder, ties her navy school sweater around her waist, casting one final glance at Greta. 'I'll ring you later.'

She catches sight of Stella across the deserted playing field, standing alone by the school gate. She's wearing dark blue jeans and a lime green t-shirt, her sun-bleached curls falling in spirals around the frames of her sunglasses.

'You're really tanned!' Sam says, as she approaches.

'It's all this being off work.'

'Are you still on holiday?'

'Until next week. Is Greta not with you?' Stella looks past her in the direction of the school building.

'She's stayed behind to have a chat with Francesca.'

'Yeah?'

'I can't tell you what about, okay?'

'D'you want to wait?'

'She might be ages.'

Stella continues to stare at the deserted school building. 'It's weird being back here.'

She follows her sister's gaze in the direction of the grey pebbledash walls. A stocky figure has appeared from one of the side doors, making its way to one of the few remaining cars in the staff parking area.

'She's still here!' Stella says, pulling a face. 'Mrs Twist!'

The blue Astra reverses, drives slowly through the school entrance and disappears down Holly Lane.

They turn away towards the underpass.

'I'd know her anywhere,' Stella groans. "I'm so glad I got out when I did.'

'It's not that bad.'

'I forgot: *you* like it!' Stella laughs.

'There's nothing wrong with it!'

'Are you staying on in the sixth form?'

She stares at the bright mural of a cartoon jungle that has recently been painted over the graffiti on the underpass walls. New words - 'Sasha 4 Neil' and 'Sharon G is a slag' - have already been scrawled over the top.

'Oh no! Tell me you're not!'

'I don't know why you're even bothering to talk to me!'

Stella grins. 'Don't be daft!'

'You left without speaking on Sunday!'

Stella looks uncomfortable. 'That was different.'

'What d'you mean?' This is her chance now.

'I remembered I was supposed to be meeting... friends, and I didn't want to leave them waiting.'

'Friends?'

'Yeah, a bunch of us were meeting in The Mandrake.'

'So if you were going there, why did you come into church?'

'I was in town, I thought I'd drop in... I don't know. A whim.' Stella shakes her head. 'Will you stop interrogating me?'

'You'll come again, won't you?'

'I doubt it.'

'But you came on Sunday. It was a sign!'

Stella grins. 'What sort of sign?'

'A sign that God's calling you back.' She must make her see it. 'Why won't you listen to him?'

'I told you-'

'Why are you blocking him?'

'Just leave it, will you?'

She can feel her eyes welling up but she mustn't cry: not here, in front of Stella. She begins to run.

She unlatches the side gate into the back garden.

Her mother is standing by the washing line, pegging up a basket-full of dripping socks. 'Sam! I wasn't expecting you this early. Is Stella with you?'

'She's just coming.' She pushes open the backdoor to the pungent odour of washing powder and cake. Her mother must be baking for the women's prayer group tomorrow afternoon. She makes her way through the beige-carpeted hallway, up the stairs to her bedroom, turning the key in the mortice lock behind her.

A few moments later, through the open window, she hears the gate click, her mother's voice: 'I won't be a minute. Put the kettle on.'

She listens to Stella's footsteps moving up the stairs, pausing on the landing outside her door: 'Sam?'

She sits, motionless.

'Are you there, Sam?'

She can't speak to her: not now, she thinks; it's too hard.

The handle is turning. 'Come on, Sam!'

'I just want to be on my own,' she says, weakly.

'Is Sam not coming down?' she hears her mother ask, in the hallway.

'Doesn't look like it.'

'I thought you were going out after school.'

'So did I.'

Sam crosses the room and peers out of the open window. The garden is in full bloom: the flowerbeds bursting with vibrant pinks and purples; the shrubbery grown so thick and the hedgerow and trees so high that it's impossible to see beyond into the neighbouring gardens. Stella and her mother appear, carrying mugs of tea; they sit on the bench in the shade. A wood pigeon is cooing from a nearby tree; a lawn mower whirrs somewhere in the distance.

'Is Sam all right?' Stella is saying.

'Why? Has something-?'

'It's... I don't know. She's so highly strung.'

'That's just Sam.' Their mother shakes her head, smiling. 'Don't forget she's had her exams - she's very determined to do well. There were all sorts of problems with Joe about that.'

'That's not... Oh, it doesn't matter.'

'Did you have a nice holiday?'

She moves away from the window. She mustn't give up with Stella, she thinks. This is a test. But 'nothing is too difficult for him', she reminds herself. She'll pray later and ask God for another chance.

Suddenly, she remembers Greta, staring down at her tight knot of fingers; Francesca perfectly composed.

She quietly unlocks the door and slips into her father's study. Picking up the telephone receiver, she dials Greta's number and waits for her familiar voice. 'It's me. How'd it go?'

'Fine.' Greta sounds distant.

'Did you tell her?'

'Mm.'

'Well, what did she say?'

'Not much.'

'You told her all of it, right?'

'Mm.'

'She must have said something!'

'She said I need to see a Christian counsellor.'

'A what?'

'A Christian counsellor,' Greta replies, flatly. 'She said there's one in the church.'

'Is there? Who?'

'I don't bloody know!'

Thirty-one

Evil

Sam hurries through the arcade into North Walk; she's already fifteen minutes late. It was her suggestion for everyone to go home and change after the exam, and meet in Giovani's at five thirty. They have to order by six o'clock to use the Happy Hour menu.

Italian guitar music jangles through the restaurant, making it seem busier than it actually is. She spots Sarah and Maria at a table in one of the alcoves; Maria is studying the menu and drinking a glass of coke through a straw.

'Sorry I'm late.'

'Where's Greta?' Maria asks, impatiently.

'She'll be here in a minute.' She glances towards the door.

She takes a seat beside Sarah, who shows her the menu.

'Good evening, ladies!' the waiter greets them is his flamboyant Italian accent. 'Your boyfriend is not with you?'

He's recognised her from last time: Joe's birthday meal. 'No.'

He lowers his voice, playfully, 'What are you doing later tonight?'

Sarah giggles; Maria looks unimpressed.

He grins, swiftly lighting the white candle wedged into the top of an empty wine bottle. 'Someone is looking for you, I think.' He gestures towards the entrance.

She turns to see Greta hurrying towards their table.

'Your friend is very beautiful,' he winks. 'But all you English girls are too thin, not like the Italian women.' He mimes the shape of a voluptuous Italian woman with his hands.

Sarah raises her eyebrows and giggles again.

'Good evening, bella,' he sings, as Greta joins the table. 'What would you like?' He pulls a notepad from his pocket, flipping it open and slipping the pen from behind his right ear.

'Pizza Americana,' Maria says, soberly. 'Sarah, you're having that too, aren't you?'

'And for you?' he turns to her.

'A Margherita pizza, please.'

'Okay. And for you, bella?' He winks at Greta.

'Hold on - can I see the menu? I'll have the same as Sam.'

'Two Pizza Margheritas. And something to drink?'

'Four cokes,' Maria says, flatly.

'Make that three,' Greta interrupts. 'I'll have a beer, please.'

Across the table, Maria is frowning.

'He was like that before,' she says, as the waiter struts off, 'when I came with Joe.'

'Do you realise,' Sarah beams around the table, 'we've actually finished!'

'Thank God!' Greta traces her finger along the congealed candle wax stuck to the side of the bottle.

'It's hard to believe, isn't it?' She's been working every day and night for so many weeks.

'How did you get on in the history exam today?' Maria asks.

Greta groans.

'I thought it was all right,' Maria persists. 'Didn't you?'

'It was okay,' she says.

'We can forget about all that,' Sarah smiles, cheerfully. 'We're on holiday now. Hey, are you going to that Martin Joseph concert Ben was talking about?'

'It's on when you lot are away at the festival,' Maria replies.

'It's not; it's the week after.'

'I'll go,' Greta says. 'Sam's got his album, haven't you?'

She nods. She bought it from the Christian Rock section in the bookshop in Park Street.

'Why don't we all go?' Sarah suggests.

Maria looks indifferent. 'What did you guys think of last night, anyway?'

The youth meeting had taken place at the Light of the World Centre and Tim, the centre manager, gave them a talk about the dangers of the occult.

'That was spooky,' Sarah shudders. 'All that stuff about ouija boards.'

'Adam's told me that thing about 'Stairway to Heaven' before,' Greta says.

'Do you think it's true? About the Satanic voices?'

'Adam said if you play the record backwards, you can hear them.'

The waiter brings across a tray with their drinks. 'Three cokes. And one beer for *you*, bella.'

The restaurant smells of freshly baked pizzas, tomatoes and garlic.

The room is like a cave, with its white, asymmetrical walls and low ceilings. Her mind flashes back to Joe's birthday: Joe ordering a bottle of wine, unwrapping the grey t-shirt she'd spent ages choosing.

'I know what I was going to tell you,' Maria says, suddenly. 'You know that new film, 'The Last Temptation of Christ'? Remember? The one Graham Weaver was talking about in the meeting on Sunday?'

Graham had told the congregation that the film was blasphemous and came from the Devil. The sort of man portrayed as Jesus was far from the perfect, beautiful man they know him to be: 'We must unite together in prayer against this evil film. I would encourage each and every one of you to take a day to fast and pray so that God will know you're serious about taking action for him.'

'I saw a report about it on the news last night,' Maria says. 'It sounds terrible.'

They nod, solemnly.

'Well, I've had an idea.' Maria looks animated. 'Why don't we write letters to the local newspapers protesting about the film being shown in all the Bristol cinemas.

Sarah's face lights up. 'I know! Why don't we fast and pray too? So the letters have more effect. We could do it tomorrow at Greta's.'

'We're meant to be organising the youth rally tomorrow,' Maria replies. 'We've still got loads to do.'

'We can do both, can't we?'

Sam takes a sip of coke. 'I think it's a good idea.'

'We could start fasting from tomorrow morning when we wake up,' Sarah continues, 'until Sunday morning. That'll give us loads of time to pray.'

'Oh my God!' Greta tops up her glass of beer from the bottle. 'I'll be starving!'

The waiter approaches their table with plates of pizzas. 'Would you like pepper?'

'Yes, please,' Greta smiles, flirtatiously. 'And could I have another beer?'

'Another one?' Maria notes, crossly.

'Why? Do *you* want one?' Greta asks.

Maria scowls and the waiter laughs.

Thirty-two

Visions

Sam slides open the top drawer of her desk, removing the leather-bound Bible. The book, with its well-thumbed, tissue-paper pages; margins covered in her small, neat handwriting; carefully underlined sections of text; bookmarks and slips of paper scrawled with jottings tucked inside the front and back covers, has become almost a part of her.

It wasn't difficult missing breakfast. Her mother keeps going on about it: 'Just a slice of toast. You can't go out without anything!'

'I'm not hungry, Mum. Those pizzas were enormous last night.'

She must prepare herself for the day ahead. They are meeting at Greta's at eleven to start praying; the attic is the ideal place.

She takes her red notebook and Bible study guide from the shelf above her desk. This week, God has been teaching her about righteous and justified anger; there are many things happening in the world that we should be angry about, she's realised: abortion, racism, low moral standards in the media.

She's copied down the example of holy anger from Exodus 32; in the passage, Moses comes down from Mount Sinai carrying the ten commandments and discovers his people worshipping idols: 'And as soon as he came near to the camp he saw the calf and the dancing. And Moses' anger blazed hot, and he cast the tablets out of his hands and broke them at the foot of the mountain. He took the calf they had made and burned it in the fire and ground it to powder and scattered it on the water and made the Israelites drink it.'

'Sometimes we must openly display our anger,' she notes down under today's date, 'e.g. The Last Temptation of Christ'. It would be wrong to sit quiet about it, she thinks. If they fast and pray hard enough, God will answer and the film will be banned.

'In him all things are possible,' she writes.

'Read it out from the beginning, will you?' instructs Maria, who's been dictating the vision.

Sam reads from the group notebook: 'All the churches in Bristol will sell their buildings and combine the money raised to buy land. A huge dome-shaped building will be built on the land, with a centre to help the poor and needy. Thousands of Christians in the city will meet here each week and begin a massive evangelical outreach in Bristol. Each person in the church must aim for a faith of high standards so that the church will be full of genuine people.'

'That's it! Perfect!' Maria looks delighted. 'Now we can see how our vision for the youth rally fits into the wider picture.'

'Can we?' Greta is lying sprawled across the floor, limp and glassy-eyed.

Irritation crosses Maria's face. 'Remember the vision we've been talking about for weeks, Greta? Our rally will be the first step to uniting the churches together.'

There is a knock on the bedroom door.

'Yes?' Greta calls.

Lou steps inside the doorway carrying a red and white cardboard box and a stack of plates. She looks ordinary today, in jeans and a t-shirt, without any make-up on; she could be a different person to the glamorous woman Sam glimpses on the way out to gigs. 'I thought you all deserved a treat. You've been stuck up here for weeks, revising or whatever it is you girls do.' She lifts the lid of the box, setting it down with the plates on the floorboards in the middle of the room. 'Help yourselves,' she smiles.

Sam inhales the unmistakable sweet scent of doughnuts; bright red sticky jam is leaking from the sugary crusts. She looks away.

'No thanks.' Maria's lips are pursed, firmly.

Sarah picks up the group notebook, flicking though the pages.

'Doesn't anyone want one?' Lou sounds offended. 'You girls need to indulge every now and again! Celebrate the end of your exams! Greta, you'll have one, won't you, darling?'

Greta shakes her head, mournfully. 'Sorry, Mum.'

'Suit yourselves,' Lou shrugs, stooping to recover the box. '*I'm going to have one with a cup of tea.*'

Once Lou has left the room, Greta looks around pleadingly. 'Come on, you guys! We've managed all morning. One won't–'

Maria's look of disdain stops her short.

Sarah picks up the list. 'So we're sending copies to Mary Whitehouse, Sir Patrick Mayhew, The British Board of Film Censors, The Observer, The Gazette, The Evening Post, ABC Cinemas,

Cannon Cinemas, Odeon cinemas, Just Seventeen. Anyone else?'

'I think that covers all of them,' Maria says.

'I don't mind typing up the letter,' Sarah offers.

'Let me read it one more time and see how it sounds.' Maria is an expert at journalistic writing after her work experience placement last summer with the Bristol Evening Post.

'Dear Sir/Madam, we are writing to express our concern over the distasteful ideas represented in the film, The Last Temptation of Christ, directed by Martin Scorcese. We have not seen this film but it has become evident through reading numerous reviews and newspaper reports that it is both blasphemous and offensive to the Christian faith.

'Words cannot describe the grief that we feel about the false suggestions portrayed in the film. But these feelings cannot be compared with those of God. His heart must contain great sorrow as he sees thousands of people flocking to watch this cruel representation of the life and ultimate sacrifice of his beloved son.

'We realise that the film companies concerned are only after money, but no amount of money could ever excuse the sin committed against God. To pass this film off lightly is pleasing the Devil. Must we have such a low standard of acceptance as to stand quiet about this? Must cinemas stoop so low just to boost their attendance figures?

'As a group of 16-year olds, we personally were horrified when first reading reviews about this film. It is due to be certified on the 9th August: we would not even consider watching it and we sincerely hope that it will not be shown in this country.'

'Wow!' Sarah beams. 'That has impact!'

'So everything's done now.' Greta has the pale, cross look she acquires when she's hungry. 'We've finished.'

'I think we should stay together till five o'clock, like we agreed, in case anyone's tempted to weaken and break the fast.' Maria glances purposefully towards Greta. 'Why don't we pray for the youth rally again?'

'D'you think we should talk to Francesca about it?' Sam suggests. She can't wait to tell Francesca all their ideas. 'Get her support.'

'I think we should,' Sarah agrees. 'Why don't we phone her now? Does anyone have her number?'

'I do.' Greta reaches for her school bag from the tangled heap of clothes at the end of the bed. 'She… gave it me, but I don't want to be the one who phones. Sam, will you do it?'

'Okay. But you'll all have to wait here.'

She perches on the stool at the rickety desk in the hallway and lifts the telephone receiver, pressing it to her ear. Clapping and cheers echo from the lounge where Lou is watching Wimbledon. Squinting down at the digits on Gretta's scrap of paper, she dials Francesca's number.

She tenses, picturing the telephone ringing in Francesca's house, Francesca getting up from the pink sofa to answer... But the phone rings, and rings, and rings...

'She wasn't there.' She tries not to let her disappointment show. 'It doesn't matter; we'll see her tomorrow.'

'I have an idea,' Sarah says. 'We'll all be leaving school after the sixth form; Greta might not even be staying on next year. We need to start thinking about the future. Let's all write down our short term visions. Greta, have you got some paper?'

This is easy for Sam: she thinks about the future all the time, her plans churned over endlessly in her journal. 'Study A levels at school,' she writes. 'Tell as many people as I can about God and keep helping Francesca with the Christian Union. Gap year helping at a Christian mission station somewhere in the world (wherever God is calling me). See where God takes me.'

'Come on, Greta.' Maria is trying to sound encouraging.

'But I just don't *know*!' Greta's piece of paper is still blank.

'You must have *some* ideas, even if you're not sure what you want to do. It's like me: I want to be a journalist or a vicar. God will tell me the right thing when it's the right time.'

'A vicar?' Greta laughs. 'Aren't vicars men?'

'Not all of them; when I went to the Methodist church camp last year, there were quite a lot of women vicars speaking.'

'I don't think I'd like to do that.'

'Obviously not! But you need to find the right thing for *you*. If you pray about it, God will tell you.'

Greta seems okay today, Sam thinks: she's acting like her normal self. At seven o'clock, her father is coming to pick them up and driving them over to Patricia Partridge's house on the other side of the shopping centre. Francesca has arranged it. Patricia is a trained Christian counsellor and she'll know exactly what Greta needs to do to get better.

Thirty-three

Counsellor

Her father has turned on the car radio to listen to the cricket scores. She usually moans at him to turn the volume down but tonight she's glad of the commentator's voice, making conversation impossible as they drive to the housing estate where Patricia Partridge lives.

She hasn't told Greta about the letter she found yesterday in the cutlery drawer. She wouldn't have read it if she hadn't caught sight of Greta's name, in bold handwriting on the edge of the fold. Quickly scanning the page, she'd seen that the letter was addressed to her father, from Kurt: 'I know how difficult it must be for Sam. We must pray for Greta to change and put our trust in the Lord.' Greta's name was also in the 'Items for prayer' list in the Ladies Group newsletter; Sam discovered it in the magazine rack last week when she was searching for the Radio Times. Greta had better not find out and think she's been talking about her behind her back.

On Wednesday night, her mother had knocked on her bedroom door. 'Sam, its Patricia Partridge on the phone. She wants to speak to you.'

'I've spoken to Francesca and she's explained the situation,' Patricia said, briskly. 'It might be a good idea if I talk with you and Greta together.'

'Yeah. Okay.'

'Perhaps the two of you would like to come round for a chat.'

Sam had never spoken to Patricia before, even though the Partridges come to church every Sunday. She's heard her parents mention their family over dinner: Patricia used to be a proper doctor but gave it up to look after their four children. Her gift is sorting out people's problems. What has Francesca said to Patricia, she wonders? An image of last Saturday forms in her mind again: the shock of dark red blood seeping from Greta's pale skin.

She and Greta hover awkwardly behind Patricia in the kitchen while she boils the kettle, swiftly organizes tea bags and milk into mugs. She should have worn her jeans, with pockets to shove her hands into.

'Richard's away, visiting a mission station in Africa, and I've asked the children to play upstairs,' Patricia glances in the direction of the staircase, 'so we won't be disturbed.' There's a stack of dirty plates in the sink, the washing machine whirs noisily: she's obviously a busy person; they're fortunate she's giving up her time to speak to them.

She has never been in such a tidy living room. The complete absence of clutter makes the space between the beige velvet armchair, where Patricia has positioned herself, and the long settee, on which she and Greta perch at either ends, seem vast. The room is dim, although it's still too early to switch the lights on. She can't see Greta unless she turns her head. She uncrosses her legs, crosses them again, reads the Denis the Menace cartoon on the side of the mug in her hand. There are thumps and squawks through the ceiling from the room above.

'So,' Patricia fixes her gaze on Greta, 'I gather you have a problem.'

The clock on the mantelpiece ticks like a drum beat; the gaudy, floral design on the curtains glares at them from across the room.

Patricia is studying Greta carefully; she wrings her hands together, over and over. Finally, she speaks, her voice crisp and doctor-like. 'It must be very difficult for your mother.'

Sam can feel her muscles tighten; her legs, where she's crossed them, are sticking together with the heat.

'What do you mean?' Greta replies.

'It must be hard for your mother, bringing up a child without a husband.'

Greta looks uneasy.

'She doesn't come to church, does she?'

'No, but...'

Sam thinks quickly. 'She's a nice person, though. Lou's great.'

Patricia gives her a sympathetic glance before focusing once more on Greta. 'You smoke, don't you?'

Greta nods and lowers her eyes to stare at the spotless cream carpet.

This isn't how Sam has expected the conversation to go. She ought to say something more, but she can't think.

Patricia sighs. 'I'll keep you in my prayers. Can I pray for you now?'

Greta nods, feebly.

Patricia shuts her eyes, purposefully. 'Lord, I bring Greta and her friend before you tonight. I pray that she will seek your forgiveness and bring her life into a place that is right with you. I ask, Lord, that you'll speak to Greta's mother; lead her out of the darkness to discover your guiding light.'

The doorbell rings. Sam's father has arranged to collect them after he's been to Tesco's.

'I ask these things in the name of Jesus. Amen.' Patricia smiles for the first time since they arrived. 'There's Pastor Loveday.'

They stand and Patricia embraces each of them stiffly. 'Come and talk again sometime. You too, Sam. This can't be easy for you.'

Sam's mouth screws into a smile.

'How was it?' her father asks, as they draw away from Patricia, waving on the doorstep.

'Okay.' She returns Patricia's wave, half-heartedly.

Greta's hands are shaking, she notices. Nobody says anything more on the drive back through the housing estate, past B&Q, the Esso garage, the red neon Tesco's sign.

She watches Greta walk up the pathway to her house, slide the key into the sky blue front door. She wants to go home, to sink into a hot bath and curl up under the duvet.

'Are you alright?' her father asks.

'Yep, fine.' She averts her eyes. The Festival of Light is less than a week away; it will all be solved there, for certain.

Thirty-four

Comfort

Greta unwraps one of the white packages, revealing a piece of fish in rock-like batter. She tears open the second package and tips the chips onto a plate, shaking out the last few that have stuck to the congealed grease on the paper.

'It was nice of him to get us some too,' Sam says.

Greta nods, taking a gulp of beer from the bottle. 'You sure you don't want one of these? Simon said we can help ourselves: there's a whole crate.'

'No thanks.' She picks up her can of Diet Coke. 'This is fine.'

Music is blaring up the stairs from the living room where Lou is entertaining her new boyfriend.

'Stevie Nicks,' Greta says. 'She always plays that album when she has a bloke round.'

'What's he like?'

'All right. He's a guitarist.' Greta takes another swig of beer. 'He seems pretty laid back.'

On the other side of the square skylight, the daylight is fading. 'Sarah phoned. She said she's posted off all the letters.'

'Oh yeah, I forgot about that.'

'I wonder if we'll get any replies.' She leans back against the red floor cushion. 'They might end up in the newspapers. Imagine that!'

Greta snaps the piece of fish into two halves, wiping her greasy fingers on her jeans. 'Help yourself.' She pulls out her silver Zippo from her pocket and crosses the room to the bookcase; she lights a joss-stick, balancing it in the soil of the spider plant, and then moves around the attic lighting candles: fat candles in dishes, rainbow candles wedged into bottle tops, tee-lights. 'Anything else happened with Joe?'

'Not since that thing with the flowers. I think he's too embarrassed to come round now.'

'Poor Joe!'

'He's not poor Joe at all! He's an idiot!'

'Only kidding! What about Matt, then?'

'I've already told you. Why've you got to keep going on about it?'

'Alright. No need to be so defensive!'

She bites into a soggy chip, trying to think of a different topic of conversation. 'I can't wait till Saturday. Dad said you and Sarah can come in our car.'

'Mm.' Greta stares at the wall, where the flickering candles light up patches of peeling wallpaper.

'What's the matter?'

'Nothing. That's great.'

The music has stopped downstairs. Greta is leaning out of the skylight, smoking a cigarette; the darkness outside is tinged by the orange glow from the streetlamp by the promenade.

She sits up stiffly, glancing at her watch. 'It's getting late. I'd better go.'

Greta continues to gaze out of the window as though she hasn't heard. She's hardly said a word for the last half an hour.

'What's up?'

'Nothing.'

'Are you okay?'

'Mm.'

'Then why didn't you phone back all week?'

'I didn't feel like talking.' Greta takes another drag from her cigarette, exhaling a long plume of smoke into the dark air.

'You look like something's wrong.'

'Do I?'

'What is it?'

'Can you stop asking me questions?'

'Is it to do with Patricia Partridge?'

'She's a silly cow!'

'Francesca can't have known what she was like, or she'd never-'

'Can we just forget it?'

'Alright.'

Greta stubs out her cigarette and lowers the skylight. 'You don't have to go. Why don't you sleep here? Mum won't mind.'

'I'd better not,' she says, getting up awkwardly. 'I haven't got any stuff with me.'

'You can borrow a t-shirt.'

'I said I wouldn't be late back.' She picks up her denim jacket from the floor.

'God, I wish Adam wasn't stuck in that place every night!' Greta says, suddenly.

'You've still not told me what's going on with you and him.'

'That's cos there's nothing to tell. He's not allowed to do anything, is he?' Greta looks utterly miserable.

'I don't know what's up with you tonight.' She sighs, sitting down again on the edge of the bed. 'Look, I'll stay over if you want.'

Rain is battering against the window. She pulls the sheet up over her shoulders; there's a draft coming from the skylight: Greta can't have shut it properly. They finished their conversation, both said goodnight, what seems like hours ago. Why can't she sleep? She should have gone home; that's what she'd wanted to do: home to her own safe bedroom, her things, Henry curled up on the end of the duvet. In the faint light from the streetlamp, she can make out Greta's hair spread across her pillow. She can tell from her breathing that she's asleep.

Trying not to make any sound, she eases herself to her feet, crossing the room to the window. A pool of water has collected on the floorboards beneath the skylight. She gently clicks it shut, glancing back at Greta: she hasn't stirred. Her head is pounding. Perhaps if she has a glass of water, that might help. Quietly, she opens the door into the hallway. She remembers that time before, when the doorbell rang in the night. But it's okay now, she comforts herself: Lou's here, and her boyfriend.

The house is silent but the lamps are still on below. She treads carefully down the flights of creaky stairs to the ground floor. The living room door is open; she runs her eyes over the pile of cassette tapes lying beside the stereo, the stack of empty bottles on the coffee table, the clothes strewn across the Persian rug. Then, catching her breath, she sees them: the hazy glow of skin; the two bodies wrapped around one another on the leather settee.

Soundlessly, she retreats hastily back up the stairs to the attic.

Thirty-five

Amazing things

Sam flicks through the glossy yellow pages of the Festival of Light programme. 'What's happening in The Big Top?'

'Celebration meetings with drama, dance and inspirational teaching,' Greta reads, from her copy of the booklet. 'But that's for older people. There's another page at the back – see? - for late teens and early twenties. It says there's meetings every morning, afternoon and evening in the Spotlight Pavilion.'

They are sitting cross-legged on the low double bed. She and Greta have said they'll share the larger bed; Sarah can have the single.

The chalet door squeaks open and Sarah appears carrying two bottles of Diet Coke. 'I found the supermarket and the canteen - it's already full of people. I think we should go.'

Even though it's gone five o'clock, the sunlight is dazzling. She fishes her sunglasses from her shoulder bag. They wander past the rows of chalets in Marina Village towards an enormous dome-shaped building; above the entrance, Waves Waterworld is printed over a blue wave. Screams echo from the glass-walled swimming pool; through the steamy glass, small wet heads and orange-arm-banded bodies bob about in the various pools, whizzing down shoots and slides. Next to the pool are red neon Burger King and Pizza Planet signs, and opposite, the amusement arcade crackles with electronic tunes and explosions.

They stop in front of the menu board outside Coral Island Food Court.

'Saturday: spaghetti bolognaise.' Greta screws up her nose. 'Great!'

'There'll be something for vegetarians,' Sam says. 'We'll ask.'

'I'm not even hungry. I'll get chips later.'

A blue plastic card with a cartoon sketch of a desert island and their chalet number has been placed at one end of their table. They're sharing with a middle-aged couple.

'Hi there!' The red-faced man shakes hands with each of them in turn across the table. 'Bill. And this is my wife, Linda.'

Linda gives them a disinterested nod and continues eating her desert: cardboardy-looking fruit crumble with a dollop of bright yellow custard

'We're from London,' Bill adds.

Sarah is sitting in the place next to him. 'I'm Sarah, and this is Sam, and Greta - from Clevedon, near Bristol.'

'Ah yes! People have come from all over. I was speaking to someone earlier from the Shetland Islands. And see that group?' He points to the nearest table with his spoon.

Sarah smiles, politely.

'They're Americans! How many Christians are at this year's festival, d'you reckon?'

Sarah shrugs.

'Must be thousands, eh! People come for all kinds of reasons.' He leans closer to their end of the table. 'So, tell me... why are *you* here?'

Greta kicks her, and Sam has to look down to stop herself laughing.

'I can't stop eating.' Bill shovels his last spoon of custard into his mouth. 'Twice as much since I gave up smoking. Put on over a stone.' He pats his stomach, bulging over his trouser belt.

When they arrived that afternoon, the Happy Parks Fun fair - the big wheel, roller-coaster, merry-go-round, go-kart track - had been buzzing with activity; now it is deserted. Everyone is dressed up for the evening, making their way across the site to the various entertainment halls and marquees. A group of young men saunter ahead of them, leaving a trail of musky cologne. It looks like they're heading in their direction, towards the Pavilion.

'I wonder if we'll bump into any of the others,' Sarah says, excitedly.

'Joe's here, isn't he?' Greta turns to her.

'I suppose so.' She is staring at the woman with the glossy auburn hair and denim jacket standing by the crazy golf kiosk: Francesca!

But the woman turns and she's disappointed: it's someone very ordinary looking, nothing like Francesca.

The Spotlight Pavilion is lit up in red lights. They make their way through the entrance doors with the sea of young people. The lights on the stage cast a warm hue across the auditorium; the band has set up across the back of the stage - the drummer in the centre, electric and bass guitarists on either side - and instrumental music blasts through the hall along with the buzz of chatter. The room is jam-packed.

She follows Sarah along one of the rows of red velvet chairs near the back.

Greta is holding onto her arm. '*How* many people?'

A young man steps into the spotlight; he is dark and suntanned, adorned in a denim jacket and a bright green t-shirt. 'Welcome to this year's Festival of Light!' he beams.

He is greeted by cheers, whistles, applause, from across The Pavilion.

'I'm Steve and I'll be leading the worship with you for the week. It's great to be here tonight! Let me introduce you to the band: the one and only Ritchie...!'

Everyone cheers as the guitar player, dressed in black, steps forward and bows. One by one, the bass player, the good looking, blond violinist (prompting ear-piercing cries and whistles), the drummer, each bow, before launching into the first song. The words appear on the OHP screen beside the stage: '*Sing and dance for joy...*' Music and singing ring around the ceiling.

Steve dances; the audience clap and dance in the aisles or where they're standing, arms waving; some make their way to the space cleared at the front.

Greta pokes her, her mouth moving to say something, then she laughs: it's impossible to hear a thing.

'Come on!' Sarah tugs her arm, pulling her towards the aisle.

'No, it's okay,' she shouts, shaking her head. 'You go.'

'This festival is now the largest Christian conference in Europe!' Steve says into the microphone before the next song. He waits for the cheering to die down before continuing, 'Last year, it was attended by more than fifty-five thousand people!'

More screams of applause.

'Now, let me put this to you: if everyone in this room tonight chooses one person to befriend, spends time getting to know that person and introduces them to Jesus, then the number of Christians here could double by this time next year! It won't be long before the whole of Britain is introduced to Jesus!'

The Pavilion explodes into shouts and clapping.

'D'you want to go to a cafe or something?' Greta says. 'It's not even ten o'clock.'

She is wide awake, but she's not in the mood for bustling rooms of people and noise.

'Can we go back to the chalet and talk?'

'Yeah, let's do that,' Sarah agrees. 'It's more private there.'

Back in the room, she pulls across the brown curtains. Maybe it's the grimy-looking orange lampshade and brown carpet: the light in the room is incredibly dim.

Sarah pours them each a plastic cup of Diet Coke and they sit cross-legged on top of the double bed. The lime woollen blankets, tucked into tight envelope corners, are scratchy on the exposed skin of her legs.

'Well, Joe wasn't there,' Greta states.

'Thank goodness.' She sips her drink.

'We might not have seen him if he was,' Sarah points out. 'There were so many people! I couldn't see anyone from the group.'

'He definitely wasn't there,' Greta says again. 'Maybe he went to the thing in the marquee; he's probably in one of the music groups. Is he playing this week, Sam?'

She shrugs. 'It's weird: I've known him two years but I don't feel like I know him at all.'

Sarah frowns. 'It must take years to really know-'

'I don't agree,' Greta interrupts. 'If you're honest, I reckon you could get to know someone really quickly - in one night even.'

'But could you trust them?' Sarah asks.

'Joe will be wherever Kurt is, obviously,' she says, thinking aloud. They probably won't see Francesca all week, she suddenly realises, her heart sinking. She's not exactly going to be at the meetings for teenagers, is she?

'I know what,' Sarah says. 'Why don't we pray together?"

'Okay.' She glances at Greta, who doesn't protest.

She closes her eyes, listening to the sounds outside: the distant hum of music from the cafes and bars, footsteps passing outside the chalet, muffled voices, a door opening and closing. 'Dear Lord,' she begins, 'thank you for bringing us here. Fill us with your power this week so that we can do amazing things for you...'

Thirty-six

Leadership

'You sure you're not coming to breakfast?' Sarah asks.

'No, you go on.' She might be able to steal some quiet time to think and pray before the Bible study at eleven o'clock.

She gazes at Greta, still in bed: it's incredible how long she can sleep. She's tugged the woollen blanket up over her ears, her tangled blonde hair splayed across the pillow.

She quietly pulls out her Next jeans and green woollen jumper from the rickety wardrobe; their clothes are squeezed onto the narrow rail: Sarah's patterned mini skirts and blouses, Greta's cotton flares and baggy jumpers.

The pokey bathroom next to the bedroom has no window; the stone floor is chilly under her bare feet. She peers into the mirror; the glass is tinted, causing her face, in the dull light, to look out of focus. She scrapes her hair back with a band and carefully smoothes mascara onto her eyelashes.

It's all going to be all right now, she thinks. 'Thank you God,' she says in her head, 'for caring for me wherever I am, and caring for the people I love.'

God has answered so many of her prayers, hasn't he? She asked him to give her friends to talk to about her faith and he gave her Greta, Sarah and Maria. He's never let her down. He hasn't always answered her prayers exactly in the way she's expected, but this is to teach her something, isn't it? To keep her in line with his plan.

She's so glad they came; the meeting last night was amazing! She pictures God on his royal throne in heaven; all around him are choirs of angels singing praises. She enters the throne room before God, the most powerful being in the whole universe, and, as she draws near to him, he reaches out to her, takes her in his arms.

"The Holy Spirit is God's power,' the speaker, Mike, tells them. 'Without the Holy Spirit, you are useless on your own. You must examine your spirituality in the same way that a school exam checks your intellectual ability or a doctor might check your physical capability.'

Sam glances along the row at Greta's and Sarah's intent faces. She thought the Bible study would take place in a small group but there must be hundreds of young people in The Stage hall. She still hasn't seen anyone from the church, though.

'You are all in different places spiritually,' Mike says, 'but however strong a Christian you are, you need to take note of what Paul says, in 1 Corinthians 10, verse 12: 'Whoever thinks he is standing firm had better be careful that he does not fall.'

She scribbles down the reference in her journal to underline neatly in her Bible later.

'I hope to see you all here again at eleven o'clock tomorrow.' Mike holds up a copy of the yellow festival programme. 'Each morning in The Real Picture, we'll be taking a look at difficult areas that you, as young people, are faced with. Tomorrow's hot topic will be 'Facing sexual issues in our modern society.''

Sarah nudges her and whispers, 'Coming?'

She nods.

'And don't forget,' Mike says, 'if you want to ask for advice about anything in your lives you're struggling with, just ask one of the leaders with a red badge. We're always ready to help: that's what we're here for.'

Sarah presses the receiver to her ear and dials Maria's number once more.

'Who spoke to you?' Sam asks.

'The waitress.' Sarah holds the ten pence coin poised, ready to press into the slot. 'She just said there was a message for our table to phone Maria Davies, urgently... The line's definitely dead. We'll have to try somewhere else.'

'I told you. None of them are working,' Greta says 'The phone by the canteen, the one outside the swimming pool. I tried to phone Adam loads of times last night.'

'We could find a phone box in Southaven,' Sarah suggests.

'Good idea,' Greta replies. 'I promised I'd call him.'

'Not to phone Adam, idiot!' Sarah shoves her. 'We have to speak to Maria. They said it's urgent!'

'We'll miss lunch if we go now,' Sam says. 'I'm starving. Why don't we go this afternoon, after the meeting?'

'Okay, but I hope she's all right. I'm dying to know what it is '

They head across the site towards the canteen.

'Hey, look!' Sarah gestures across the busy street in the direction of The Quay House, the VIP restaurant.

Through the crowds, she spots Kurt and Francesca walking towards the glass swinging door.

They hurry to catch up, but just as they are almost within reach, Sarah grabs her elbow, pulling her back.

'You have no idea!' Kurt is saying, his voice raised. He hasn't noticed them approaching behind. 'These aren't just little youth workers that nobody's even heard of! These are the directors of the whole damn organisation! You know they've asked me to speak this afternoon.'

'It's *you* who's on the leadership team. I don't even know them!'

'Then it's about time you did!'

'What if I don't want to?'

He raises his hands in the air abruptly, causing Francesca to step back, almost crashing into them.

'I'm a leader at this festival,' Kurt is ranting, red faced, 'so that means you are too! Like all the other wives.' He grips hold of Francesca's arm and marches her into the restaurant.

'Blimey!' Greta raises her eyebrows.

They gaze through the glass doors as he steers her towards a long table where a group are seated by the window. The Quay House diners seem different to those in their canteen: well-groomed men in shirts and ties, women in floral skirts and sensible blouses. Faces look up as Kurt and Francesca take the two empty chairs at the end of the table.

The main street is lined with cafes, fish and chip shops, gift shops with racks of postcards, inflatable lilos and dinghies hanging outside.

'Can we pop in here a minute?' Greta moves towards the door of a shop, The Enchanted Sun: one of those places selling incense and ethnic jewellery.

'We need to find a phone box,' Sam reminds her, or we'll be late for supper, and I want to go back and change before the meeting tonight.'

'There's one.' Sarah points towards The Royal Hotel across the street.

They squeeze inside the red phone box outside the hotel. It reeks of stale cigarettes. Sam rummages through her purse, retrieving a fifty pence piece.

Sarah dials the number, holding the receiver to her ear. 'It's ringing...' She grabs the coin and shoves it into the machine. 'Maria? It's Sarah!'

Greta is miming inhaling on a cigarette behind Sarah's back. She won't smoke in front of Sarah, though. Sam would like it to be just herself and Greta for a bit, to talk. She's desperate to ask her what she thinks of that thing with Kurt and Francesca earlier.

'No...! Really?' Sarah moves the phone away from her mouth, grinning. 'The letter's in the newspaper! The Bristol Evening Post!' She presses the phone to her ear again. 'She says it's been shortened but the message still comes across power-'

'Ask her to get us copies,' Sam interrupts.

'Hang on... Wow!'

'What?'

'It's in The Gazette as well! Printed in full!'

Thirty-seven

Holy Spirit

'Yoohoo!... Girls!' Mr. Tippet's voice booms, from the direction of the tinned foods aisle.

They have popped into the Happy Parks supermarket, to purchase some shower gel to replace the brittle square of soap in their chalet. Sam turns away from the household goods section, trying not to show her alarm: she has just noticed, dangling from the rack beside the men's deodorants, the plastic packages of razors. Greta registered them at the same time and averted her eyes. Mr. Tippets is hurrying towards them, waving frantically.

She eyes his basket of groceries: vacuum packed bacon; a tin of ravioli; a packet of Custard Creams.

'We've been looking everywhere for you,' he puffs, red-faced. 'We were beginning to think we'd never find you. Where have you been?'

'The youth meetings.' She scans the shop over his shoulder: no Francesca.

'Ah yes! Well, Francesca and I have been going to the Big Top celebrations. Fabulous! The marquee holds four thousand and it's full every night!'

Francesca and I? *Why,* Sam thinks, would someone as amazing as Francesca want to spend the holiday with *him*?

'Where are you staying?' Mr. Tippets continues.

'Marina Village,' Sarah replies. 'It's by the indoor swimming pool.'

'We're in the self-catering block in Ocean Village, just over there.' He points vaguely towards the block of buildings opposite. 'Why don't you come and have a cup of tea?'

They traipse after him along streets of white-washed chalets, up a wooden staircase, along a boarded walkway; he stops outside one of the blue doors, rummaging for the key in his trouser pocket (the too-short trousers that he wears for school).

The layout of his chalet is similar to theirs, except for the small kitchen unit under the window. The two single beds are covered in the same scratchy, lime blankets.

'I don't know where Francesca is.' Mr. Tippets tries to make himself heard over the rumble of the kettle boiling. 'She went off to the Bible study earlier.'

The three of them are seated in a line on one of the beds; they've left the blue plastic chair free for Mr. Tippets.

'Is she staying...?' Sam glances at the bed behind her. 'I mean-'

'She's not staying here!' He lets out an uncharacteristic chuckle. 'Francesca and Kurt have the chalet next door. Kurt's out with the leadership most of the time, so I'm able to keep her company.' He chuckles again.

Greta nudges her behind her back.

'What about the youth meetings? Are you enjoying yourselves?' He slops hot water and milk into four glass mugs, the same sort of mugs that are used in the dining hall. His sandaled feet are small and hairy, she notices, and look incongruous poking out of the ends of his science teacher trousers.

'They're brilliant,' Sarah says.

'Oh good! And the after-parties? I read about those in the brochure. Sounds like fun.'

Sarah shakes her head. 'There's so much to take in. In the evenings, we've gone back to the chalet and just talked about it all really, and prayed together.'

Mr. Tippets nods, 'Jolly good stuff!'

'We've learnt some new songs in the meetings,' Sarah adds. 'We've bought the Festival of Light Praise Book so we can sing them in Christian Union.'

'Oh yes!' he beams. 'I'll tell Francesca!'

They could hear the rock band start in the Spotlight Pavilion from the other side of the Prize Bingo hall. They squeeze past a row of people, smiling apologetically, to take what looks like the last three seats available together. She doesn't mind singing here, with the loud speakers blasting out music from the electric guitars and drums at a deafening volume; dark, handsome Steve leading the thousands of young people singing, '*We'll march across the nation with hearts on fire...*,' hands stretched high in the air.

Sarah raises her hands and dances, her assortment of multi-coloured bracelets jingling up and down her arms.

She wants, desperately, to be among those dancing and praising God more freely but, for some reason, she can't. She and Greta are the only ones in the room not worshiping whole-heartedly, the only ones putting themselves first and blocking God. Greta hovers awkwardly beside her, her black t-shirt-clad arms hugging her chest.

'*Let the fires blaze across this darkened land; let them blaze! let them blaze!*'

The musicians improvise: the violin, saxophone, flute, keyboard and guitar players creating their own chords and melodies. Steve speaks in tongues, dynamically, into the microphone. All around the auditorium, people raise their hands and pray aloud.

Her eyes move to the woman sitting a couple of rows down; the woman's hair and complexion are golden, her shoulders slender, but, of course, it can't be her. She'll be in the Big Top with Mr Tippets. Besides, the woman's posture isn't as elegant as Francesca's. She glances at Greta beside her: her eyes are closed, her pale eyelids giving away nothing of her thoughts, her arms folded around herself.

'I used to tell people,' blond Pete says into the microphone, 'when they were being filled with the Holy Spirit, to imagine themselves as a beaker filling up with water. Then, one day, God said to me, 'What's the use in that? Just sitting there passively.' Now I tell people to imagine themselves as a long hosepipe attached to a tap.' He grins out across the Pavilion. 'When God fills them with the Holy Spirit, water bursts from the tap, gushing through the hose and out the end. Spraying people's lives with Jesus!'

'Thank you, Pete.' Steve pats the speaker on the back as they exchange positions in the spotlight. 'I'd like to ask anyone who wants to be filled with the Holy Spirit tonight, or receive more spiritual gifts, to come forward to the front now.'

The musicians play 'Rule Over Me' softly; those left in their seats sing quietly as people all around the building shuffle past knees along rows, making their way down the aisles to stand in the space cleared in front of the stage. The team of young men and women with red badges move amongst them, heads bowed, whispering confidentially, laying hands over them.

'Fill me with the spirit, God,' Sam prays, inside her head. 'I know I've failed you. Please God, make me into a different person.'

Thirty-eight

Tongues

She passes the supermarket entrance, retracing their steps along the streets of white chalets. She doesn't have long: she told the others she was just going to have a quick look in the book tent. It seemed easier than trying to explain. She won't ask Francesca about it straight away. She'll tell her about their letter in The Gazette first: how it was inspired by the Holy Spirit and God's going to use it to speak to people. She could mention the letter in her Bible message, she thinks, when she speaks at the youth rally. She'll show them how spiritual she is, won't she...? If she can just be sure that she *is* filled with the Holy Spirit...

'Shhh!' The voice is coming from the balcony above, outside Francesca's chalet.

A door clicks shut and a woman - Pippa Bright from the youth group - appears on the stairway, her hair looking even more bleached than usual. She's wearing heavy make-up, gold jewellery, a loose white shirt worn over leggings and gold sandals.

Sam opens her mouth to speak but Pippa bristles past her, without so much as a glance, and is gone.

Maybe Pippa didn't notice her, she thinks, although how can she not have seen her? She should give up now; she has no desire to communicate with Kurt. But she knocks, sheepishly, on the blue chalet door.

Kurt answers, wearing a white towelling robe, his hair dishevelled. 'Oh… Sam!' His expression transforms into a slow grin. 'What can I do for you?'

Over Kurt's shoulder, items of clothing are strewn across the floor. The air reeks unpleasantly of sweat. There's a bottle of Jack Daniels whisky on the table. Lou keeps a bottle in her drinks cupboard. Greta tried to persuade her to have some with her one night, but the smell turned her stomach and she couldn't swallow it. Greta had made fun of her: 'Come on! Don't be a baby!'

She attempts a smile. 'I've just seen Pippa. I'm… looking for Francesca.'

'She went to a meeting with the teacher.' He gestures vaguely towards the chalet next door. 'When you find her, don't mention

Pippa, okay? She's been having a few problems and she wouldn't like to think people were talking about her.'

'Okay.' She steps back against the railing. 'See you, then.'

She has swallowed the limp slivers of cucumber and lettuce from her plate, pushed the dried-up oven chips to the side, picked at the edge of the rubbery beefburger.

She catches the attention of a waitress wearing one of the green and white catering overalls. 'Excuse me? Could I have a cup of tea, please?'

'Me too,' Greta pushes away the last half of her plate of chips and ketchup.

'So, girls...' Bill leans towards Greta. 'You're very quiet today. What's been going on in the youth meetings?'

None of them wants to take up the conversation; even Sarah has no reply.

Sam notices, with alarm, that Greta's face is growing paler and her eyes are filling up. Why doesn't he just leave them alone?

'You're not filled with the Holy Spirit, are you?' Bill says then, continuing to fix his gaze pointedly on Greta.

Greta's cheeks are streaked with tears.

'You can always tell,' he says.

'Come on,' Sam murmurs. 'We've finished.'

'I'll just have desert.' Sarah gestures towards Linda's bowl of jam rolypoly. 'I'll catch you up.'

'Does that man ever shut up?' Sam says, as they walk away from the dining hall. 'Imagine what it must be like for his wife!'

They sit in the sun, on the patch of grass in front of the row of chalets. The boys from the block next to theirs have brought a ghetto blaster outside and they're playing UB40, sprawled lazily on the grass, drinking cans of beer. Greta produces a packet of Embassy No 1, offering it to her: it's almost empty.

'No thanks.'

Greta lights a cigarette and leans towards the boys. 'Any chance of a beer over here?'

The mousy-haired one tosses her a can.

'Cheers.' Greta throws him a cigarette.

'You okay?' Sam asks.

'I need to buy some more cigs.'

'That was weird seeing Mr Tippets today, wasn't it?'

'He's such a geek.' Greta pings back the ring pull; the brown liquid fizzes over the edge of the can onto the grass. She takes a swig and inhales deeply on her cigarette.

'I wonder why Francesca likes him.'

'She doesn't like him.'

'D'you think she doesn't?'

'You're so slow sometimes! It's really obvious!'

'Why does she spend time with him, then?'

Greta exhales a plume of smoke. 'Cos he goes to Christian Union and all that. You're so dim!'

She wants to tell Greta about Kurt this afternoon - about Pippa. What was she doing in his chalet? But that would mean explaining...

She tests the temperature as the water swirls into the bath tub. The room is filling with steam, leaving a film of condensation over the mirror. She tugs the brown curtain across the window, blocking out the black evening.

She unfastens her watch, peels off her clothes and lowers her body into the warm liquid. No one thought to bring bubble bath and she feels strangely naked in the clear water. She reaches to slide the plastic shower curtain across, enclosing the narrow space around herself and the water. The chrome taps are faintly outlined in the dim light. Through the wall, she can hear the muffled sound of the others talking. There is music coming from somewhere outside, maybe from the bars beside the swimming pool. She is beginning to get a sore throat; her head is throbbing. If she were at home, her mum would give her an aspirin tablet; none of them has brought anything like that. She ought to go to that supermarket tomorrow and get some.

She slips her shoulders down until the water covers her ears, trying to shut out what happened in the meeting tonight. She'd asked God to help her speak in tongues again, and there was still nothing. She knows it's because she's not right with God. If she didn't have a problem, she'd be doing it by now, like everyone else. She could try speaking to one of those leaders with the red badges. But they don't even know her, do they?

She rubs the brittle bar of soap onto the wash cloth and scrubs her skin. There's nothing else for it: she has to speak to her. Tomorrow she must find Francesca. 'Father, I promise I'll put you before everything,' she prays, in her head. 'Help me let the Holy Spirit in and fill me with your power to speak in tongues tomorrow. Amen.' She lowers her body down further under the murky water.

Thirty-nine

Saviour

'Coming into Southaven?' Sarah asks, as they make their way out of The Pavilion.

Sam doesn't reply.

Greta shrugs, miserably.

'Come on! We can go to that jewellery shop you saw the other day. Remember, Greta?'

Greta nods, compliantly.

'I...' She makes an instant decision. 'I just need to speak to someone a minute. I'll catch up with you.'

Sarah casts her a meaningful look. 'See you later, then.'

She watches Greta trailing behind Sarah, out through the doors at the back of the hall. The building is clearing; there are only a few young people left at the front receiving prayer. She hurries towards the entrance on the other side; she must get to the Big Top before the afternoon meeting finishes.

She sees her before she reaches the marquee, walking in the direction of the Ocean Village chalets. She's wearing sunglasses, an elegant silvery grey skirt. Mr. Tippets is nowhere in sight, thank goodness. God is giving her a sign, she is sure. There's only one person who can help her now.

Francesca lifts her sunglasses, resting them on top of her head. 'Okay if we sit here?'

She nods. Francesca has taken her into a bar area at the back of an entertainment hall she doesn't recognise. The room is deserted; there is just enough light coming in through the doors to see by.

'This is where they have the Meditation Bible studies,' Francesca says.

They sit on the faded, red velvet seats at one of the round tables. She feels incredibly stupid all of a sudden; perhaps she shouldn't have asked her. Everyone else is managing to cope.

'What is it you want to talk to me about?' Francesca asks, her voice measured.

She looks different today, Sam thinks: paler, although, in the muted light, she can't see her face clearly. She's not wearing make-up: is that it? Her mind seems to have gone blank; she can't remember any of the things she's planned to say.

'Are you worried about Greta??'

'Er yeah… I am…'

Francesca nods, sympathetically.

'But it's not just that,' she adds, quickly.

Francesca tugs her fingers through her hair. It looks more tussled and uncombed than usual.

'I can't - I keep trying - but I can't speak in tongues… I… think I might not be filled with the Holy Spirit.' She is glad of the darkness; her hands and upper lip have started to shake. She pushes her palms into the cushioned seat to keep them still.

'Can you talk to anyone about how you feel?' Francesca says, calmly.

'I can talk to Greta about some things.'

'That's good. I often feel bad too, so I understand.' Francesca's voice is reassuring. 'The first thing I suggest you do is make a list of the good things about yourself.'

'Okay.'

'And another list of the things you like doing.'

'I was wondering… would you pray for me to be able to speak in tongues?' She looks down at the brown swirls in the carpet, at Francesca's elegant sandals, her silver-painted toe-nails. She feels so clumsy.

'Sure.' Francesca reaches across the table for one of her hands, holding it loosely between her fingers. It's too close; she can hardly breathe.

She closes her eyes and tries to stop her hand from shaking; she must act normal. She shouldn't have come to find her, shouldn't have said anything.

'Have you ever spoken in tongues before?' Francesca asks, softly.

'No, I don't think so.'

'Okay… Lord, I pray that you will fill Sam with your spirit… I ask that she'll be able to speak in tongues, right here, today.'

It's her turn. The blood rushes to her head, like it did in the meeting this afternoon, only this is worse because Francesca is sitting only an inch away, holding her hand, waiting.

'Are you stuck?'

She nods, sombrely, opening her eyes. Francesca's face is shadowed.

'Start by saying a letter. Any letter.'

She lowers her eyelids again. 'K.'

'And another letter?'

'Y.' The cushioned seat is unbearably lumpy, her back aching.

'And another.'

'S.'

'Now use the letters as beginnings of words. Just open your mouth and let the words come out.'

She does: she hears herself speak a whole string of strange words. Francesca slides her hands away. 'That's good.'

She opens her eyes blearily, quickly retracting her shaky hand from the table, tucking it into the safety of her jeans pocket. Francesca is a hazy silhouette, sitting further back from the table now.

'Thanks.' Her voice comes out in a whisper.

'Is there anything else I can do for you?'

'No… thanks.'

Forty

Suffering

Outside the building, the daylight is horribly bright. Wild Wickies Beach Bar - with its saloon-style bar stools and cubicles - is chaotic, with the queue for hot dogs spilling out into the street. She buttons up her khaki mac; she found it in the Oxfam shop in Clevedon a couple of months ago and it is comfortingly oversized. Greta purchased a similar one in navy. If they wear the macs with the collars turned up, it makes them look French, Greta said. She wants to cry but she mustn't, not here. She digs her hands deep into her pockets, turning off the main path into a quieter street of chalets. The blocks of white-painted wooden buildings, row upon row of red doors and red-framed windows, all look the same. She feels as though people are watching her through the chalet windows.

Hastily, she takes a turning back in the direction of the electronic whirrs and jingles, the children's shrieks from the fairground and the outdoor pool.

The posters along the walls advertise 'Party party party', '70s Glitternight', 'Karaoke', 'Celebrity Weekend': activities taking place on normal weeks later in the summer. She slips inside the nearest gift shop, focusing her attention on the racks of pink sticks of rock, the candy dummies and red heart-shaped lollipops. She could look for presents for her parents, she thinks, scanning the wicker baskets of novelty key-rings, cuddly toys, tea towels with maps of Southaven.

Outside again, she looks around, checking there's no-one about from the church: she doesn't want to talk to anyone. That supermarket might have presents, she thinks: toffee for her dad, clotted cream fudge for her mum. Stella's not keen on sweet things, though. She's not seen her sister for ages, has she?

She's beginning to well up again but she stops abruptly. At the far end of the street, Greta has appeared through the double doors to the supermarket; she is walking rapidly in the opposite direction, her denim jacket and blonde flyaway hair unmistakable. Gathering herself together, she hurries after her.

When Sam reaches the chalet, the curtains have been pulled across.

She pushes her key into the lock, turns it and opens the door with a shove.

Greta is standing beside the double bed with her back to the door. She twists her head around, her expression startled. 'Sam!'

'What're you doing?'

'I thought you were talking to someone.'

'I thought you were going into Southaven with Sarah.'

Greta still hasn't turned around. 'I didn't feel like it.'

'What've you got in your hand?'

Greta stares at her.

'What's in your hand?'

'...Can't you just leave me alone?'

'Why? What's the matter?' She steps across the room to where Greta is standing, awkwardly covering her left hand with her right.

As Greta opens her palm, something shiny falls to the floor.

Her stomach clenches; 'Ugh!'

'I did tell you…'

Greta's cupped hand is swimming with blood, dark and red. It runs down her arm, dripping onto the carpet.

'How…?'

'I'm stupid, okay? There's tissues in the pocket of my suitcase.'

Sam yanks the suitcase out from the bottom of the wardrobe; there's a packet of Kleenex stuffed into the side pocket, along with a yellow tube of antiseptic cream, a reel of cotton bandage. 'You came prepared!' She begins wrapping the tissues, one at a time, around Greta's palm, trying not to wince as the red fluid rapidly saturates the white paper. 'What am I meant to do now?'

'Sorry! Better run it under the cold tap.'

She steers Greta into the bathroom.

'Don't tell Sarah.'

She turns on the tap, checks the temperature, steadying Greta's wound under the stream of water. 'Does it hurt?'

'Stinging. How long is it before supper?'

'About half an hour.'

'I want a cig before Sarah gets back.'

'Okay,' she sighs. 'I'll come with you.' She turns off the tap, reaching for the bandage. 'But we need to be quick.'

'Wait.' Greta reaches with her other hand into her sweatshirt pocket. 'Would you get rid of these?' She hands over a small packet of blades, torn open at the top.

'So…' Bill shovels a forkful of mashed potato into his mouth as though he's not eaten for a week. He's already polished off Linda's portion of roast potatoes. 'Just two days to go.'

'Mm,' Sarah mutters.

Greta is staring towards the windows on the far side of the canteen. Her bandaged hand is hidden under the table, covered by the cuffs of her Indian cotton shirts.

'It's been fabulous, hasn't it?' Bill swallows another great heap of potato. 'Nothing else like it!'

Linda ignores her husband, her attention engaged with negotiating her plate of chicken, carrots, and peas.

'What've you done to your hand, Sam?' Bill grins, chewing energetically.

'I fell over. And I'm not Sam,' Greta says, flatly.

'Oops! Sorry love! I'm terrible with names.'

'No worries,' Greta replies, absently.

'The celebration tonight should be something else! I can't wait! Last night they had us singing 'Jesus walks the land in radiance.' Do you know that one? Everyone marching around the tent. I'm surprised you didn't hear us!'

Sam's headache and sore throat are growing worse, but she mustn't be ill. No way is she going to miss any of the meetings, especially not after this afternoon. She hasn't told Greta and Sarah about what happened with Francesca yet; she needs time to explain it properly. She'll save it for tonight, when they talk after the meeting.

Forty-one

Lost

'Where's Greta?' Sarah asks, as they watch the latecomers disappearing through the entrance to the Spotlight Pavilion. The band is already playing.

'Typical!' Unlike Greta, Sam made sure she remembered to take her Bible with her to supper so she wouldn't have to traipse all the way back to the chalet before the meeting.

The sun is still blazing, the sky a vibrant blue. The last remaining groups, chattering in high spirits, hurry from the chalets, the book tents, the restaurants, to the various celebration venues dotted across the Happy Parks complex. An image of her sister forms in her mind: she pictures her here, in the hustle and bustle, wearing the lime green t-shirt and jeans she had on that day at the school gate, sunglasses perched on her sun-bleached curls.

'Stella!' she would say. 'What're you doing here?'

'I can't explain it but I felt something calling me to the train station, something telling me to take a trip down here for the day.'

'Which celebration are you going to?' If Stella went to just one meeting, she'd have to see it; she wouldn't be able to leave without giving her life back to God. 'The youth meeting's brilliant – and there's loads of others. Francesca goes to-'

'You sure Greta knows where to find us?' Sarah interrupts her thoughts.

She nods. 'She *must* know the doughnut stall - we walk past it every day.'

'Maybe she missed us; maybe she's already gone in.'

'She can't have.' She squints in the sunlight, lifting her hand to shade her eyes. There are still a few people scattered along the maze of pathways, making their way to events. 'I wonder what the other meetings are like.'

'Ours are the best,' Sarah states.

'The Big Top sounds pretty good too, from what Francesca said.'

'Francesca?' Sarah turns to look at her. 'Have you seen her?'

She smiles. 'I'll tell you about it later with Greta-'

'It's nearly an hour since we came out of the dining hall!'

She stares at her watch, the realisation suddenly dawning on her. Sarah laughs. 'What?'

'Wait here, will you?' she calls over her shoulder, hastening in the direction of the chalet.

She hurries past the fairground, Waves Waterworld and Pizza Planet. By the time she reaches the chalets, there's not a person in sight. Why didn't she tell someone about Greta this afternoon? She could have gone to find Francesca again, asked her what to do. But she'd given her word to Greta, hadn't she?

'You won't say anything, will you? Promise you won't.'

She just needs to find her, she thinks; everything will be all right.

She halts outside the brown door. The curtains are drawn across at the window. She slides the key into the lock. 'Greta?' Her voice comes out small and strained.

There's no reply.

She enters the dimly lit room. Her eyes quickly scan the silhouetted beds, the pile of clothes strewn across the side where Greta sleeps, the red journal on the bedside table, the wardrobe, the plastic chair. The door to the bathroom is slightly ajar. Tentatively, she pushes it, but no Greta.

She stops for breath outside the supermarket. Greta's not in the dining hall and she hasn't been in the shop: the woman serving seemed sure. Where else have they been this week? There's the meetings in the Spotlight Pavilion and that other place, The Stage, but Greta can't have gone into either of those without passing them.

Her eyes start to fill up. She should have done something more to help her, and now it's too late. She should have believed more..., believed that God would heal her. But she did try, didn't she? Tears begin streaming down her face; she can't stop them.

She sits on the bench beside the candy floss stand, her hands covering her face. All the time Greta's been there for *me,* she thinks. Every day. What if she's dead?

The sun has lowered in the sky, the sharp air penetrating through the tie-dye t-shirt Greta made for her: she should have worn something warmer. The sound of a siren wails across the blue sky from the direction of the site entrance on the other side of the fairground.

The ambulance is parked in the street ahead. A group of onlookers have gathered outside the Prize Bingo hall opposite. As she approaches, two men in green uniforms slam the white rear doors of the vehicle and the deafening sirens start up again as it races away towards the gates, its red and blue lights flashing. A cry escapes from her mouth as she turns away, palms pressed against her knees.

All of a sudden, there's someone at her side. She looks up to see Greta, and she starts to laugh. 'Where *were* you?' she chokes, limply. 'I've been looking everywhere!'

'I was walking back to the hall and a woman ran out of that building.'

Greta is shaking, she notices, as her laughter subsides.

'She was yelling for someone to help.'

She follows Greta's gaze towards the glass doorway where the ambulance was parked.

'I went after her. It's a gym for adults. A swimming pool. I didn't even know it was there.' Greta glances at her momentarily then looks away.

'What happened?'

'It was too late...'

'What d'you mean?'

Greta shakes her head.

She clutches hold of the railings; something is horribly wrong. 'What're you talking about?'

'Francesca.'

Everything is growing dark and blurry.

Forty-two

A new beginning

'*He gave up his life to set us free…*' The music blares through the tiled bathroom floor from the living room below.

Ever since one of the elders gave her father a cassette recording of 'The Festival of Light Live!' he's played it every Sunday morning, singing along in the kitchen whilst peeling the potatoes and chopping the carrots for the Sunday roast.

Sam peers at her reflection in the circular bathroom mirror. She dabs the make-up brush into the rose-coloured compact, flicking it lightly over her face. How can he keep playing those songs from the festival, she thinks, fighting the urge to dash downstairs and switch it off; she can't stand it a minute longer. Every time she hears that tape, it all comes flooding back. Do her parents have no idea? She slides the cap off the Claret lipstick that she bought from John Lewis yesterday.

'Have you seen the Bristol Evening Post?' she'd asked her mother, over breakfast. 'There's an article about Francesca.'

'Such a terrible accident.' Her mother got up to put the kettle on. 'I forgot to tell you, Stella phoned. It's lovely to see you two close again.'

When she'd mentioned Kurt to her father, his mouth had tightened. 'Nick and Sarah came to the leadership meal on Friday night – a very nice couple!'

She hadn't known what to say when Sarah told her, out of the blue, that Nick was her boyfriend; she hadn't seen that coming. Nick's nice enough, she thinks, but so square! Not at all like Scott, Sarah's ex, with his leather jacket, tattoos and earrings.

'Nick's an interesting young man, isn't he?' her father had continued. 'I had a long chat with him at the meal. He's happy to stand in until the new leaders arrive. I told him he should think about Bible College, training as a youth worker: they'd love him there, with all his ideas. Who would have thought of setting up a church football team?'

'Mm.'

'And he told me he's organising a skiing trip this winter for you

The ambulance is parked in the street ahead. A group of onlookers have gathered outside the Prize Bingo hall opposite. As she approaches, two men in green uniforms slam the white rear doors of the vehicle and the deafening sirens start up again as it races away towards the gates, its red and blue lights flashing. A cry escapes from her mouth as she turns away, palms pressed against her knees.

All of a sudden, there's someone at her side. She looks up to see Greta, and she starts to laugh. 'Where *were* you?' she chokes, limply. 'I've been looking everywhere!'

'I was walking back to the hall and a woman ran out of that building.'

Greta is shaking, she notices, as her laughter subsides.

'She was yelling for someone to help.'

She follows Greta's gaze towards the glass doorway where the ambulance was parked.

'I went after her. It's a gym for adults. A swimming pool. I didn't even know it was there.' Greta glances at her momentarily then looks away.

'What happened?'

'It was too late…'

'What d'you mean?'

Greta shakes her head.

She clutches hold of the railings; something is horribly wrong. 'What're you talking about?'

'Francesca.'

Everything is growing dark and blurry.

Forty-two

A new beginning

'*He gave up his life to set us free…*' The music blares through the tiled bathroom floor from the living room below.

Ever since one of the elders gave her father a cassette recording of 'The Festival of Light Live!' he's played it every Sunday morning, singing along in the kitchen whilst peeling the potatoes and chopping the carrots for the Sunday roast.

Sam peers at her reflection in the circular bathroom mirror. She dabs the make-up brush into the rose-coloured compact, flicking it lightly over her face. How can he keep playing those songs from the festival, she thinks, fighting the urge to dash downstairs and switch it off; she can't stand it a minute longer. Every time she hears that tape, it all comes flooding back. Do her parents have no idea? She slides the cap off the Claret lipstick that she bought from John Lewis yesterday.

'Have you seen the Bristol Evening Post?' she'd asked her mother, over breakfast. 'There's an article about Francesca.'

'Such a terrible accident.' Her mother got up to put the kettle on. 'I forgot to tell you, Stella phoned. It's lovely to see you two close again.'

When she'd mentioned Kurt to her father, his mouth had tightened. 'Nick and Sarah came to the leadership meal on Friday night – a very nice couple!'

She hadn't known what to say when Sarah told her, out of the blue, that Nick was her boyfriend; she hadn't seen that coming. Nick's nice enough, she thinks, but so square! Not at all like Scott, Sarah's ex, with his leather jacket, tattoos and earrings.

'Nick's an interesting young man, isn't he?' her father had continued. 'I had a long chat with him at the meal. He's happy to stand in until the new leaders arrive. I told him he should think about Bible College, training as a youth worker: they'd love him there, with all his ideas. Who would have thought of setting up a church football team?'

'Mm.'

'And he told me he's organising a skiing trip this winter for you all, to the Alps.'

The doorbell rings in the hallway. That will be Millie Jenkins and her daughter, Abigail: her father gave them a lift to church last week. She overheard her mother on the phone yesterday: 'We can take you every Sunday. It's no problem: there's space in the car.'

She doesn't care; Greta hasn't been to church for weeks. She's hardly seen her at all since she started in the sixth form and Greta began working shifts behind the bar in Body Bliss Fitness. Sam cycled along the sea front to see her at work a couple of weeks ago.

'It's fab,' Greta said. 'I get to talk to people all night and everyone buys me drinks. And it's not just gym people... It gets really busy in the evenings when it's warm – everyone sits outside by the beach. And some nights there's lock-ins – that's such a laugh! Honestly, Sam, you should come along one night at the end of my shift.'

'So you don't miss school, then?'

Greta laughs. 'What d'you think?'

'You seem like you're doing really well.'

Greta nods, cheerfully. 'Mark said he's going to make me deputy bar manager when Julie leaves next month. That means I'll be in charge of meals as well when it's my shift.'

'That's great!'

'Can I get you a drink? Why don't you have half a cider and black? I'll have one with you.' Greta glances at the clock behind the bar. 'It won't be busy 'til about nine.'

'No, it's all right – I'd better go. I've got some homework I need to finish for tomorrow.'

The music has stopped, replaced with the sounds of voices in the living room. Millie arrives far too early, unlike Greta, who was always holding them up, having run the five minute walk between Marine Road and Trenchard Street.

She's wearing the cream silk blouse that she purchased from Next with Stella yesterday, with her long black skirt and tights, black high heels. She slips the new gold necklace from her jewellery box and fastens the clasp at the back of her neck. After they'd finished shopping, her sister had taken her for lunch in a restaurant by the docks and presented her with the necklace, wrapped in gold tissue paper. 'Here you go. A late birthday present.'

'But you've already given me a present.'

'I'm allowed to give you another one if I want to.'

Stella was only attempting to make her feel better: she knows that. Her sister had taken her out a couple of weeks after the festival and tried to ask her about it – she'd read about the death in the newspaper.

'Are you okay? It must have been a shock – that woman, Francesca, drowning herself like that.'

'Yeah,' she began, but immediately clammed up.

'And who was it her husband ran away with?'

'Pippa.'

Stella shrugged. 'I don't know her. I'm not surprised, though: he seemed the type.'

She squirts Panache onto each wrist, tucks the tube of lipstick into the pocket of her skirt and hurries downstairs.

'I have the pleasure, this morning, of introducing you to a new couple who will be joining our congregation: Julian and Beth Fletcher.' Pastor Loveday looks fresh in his pale grey suit and pastel yellow tie. 'They're coming to us from the London City Mission, where they've been working for the past three years with homeless young people. I'd like to give them a very warm welcome into our congregation.'

The museum hall, bathed in late September sunlight, resounds with applause as the couple make their way up the steps to the platform to stand beside the pulpit.

'Julian and Beth will be taking over the youth work here with us. They bring years of expertise of working with the young, and I know they're greatly looking forward to the opportunity to continue God's work in this particular field. Nick and Sarah, who you all know, are going to work with them over the coming weeks to show them the ropes and help them settle in.'

Sam glances sideways along the back row, where the young people are seated, their eyes fixed on the platform. Sarah and Nick are holding hands. Maria's not here this morning – she must have gone to the Methodist Church again. 'It suits me more,' she'd told Sam, after a week away at Methodist camp at the end of August. They're both in Mrs Clark's boring English classes at school but they don't sit together. They've not mentioned the youth rally again; there's no point. Neither of them wants to carry on with it.

It's so strange, she thinks, how nobody talks about Kurt and

Francesca now, ever; it's as though none of it ever happened. Of course, she and Greta talked it over at the time. The police had said the drowning was deliberate. But why? Neither of them could understand why she might do something like that. Francesca had so much, she thinks, controlling the desire to cry, but she won't let herself, not here in church.

Robin might understand, she thinks, glancing along the row at his pale, thin face. But he always disappears straight after the services without speaking. He'd been going out with Pippa since he finished on the rehab programme. There's a rumour going around that he's started mixing with some unsavoury characters in St Pauls.

The new leader, Julian, smiles, casual in his orange and blue checked shirt. He's small and slight, as though he could be an athlete. His wife is a short woman with dark bobbed hair; she's wearing a floral dress. She's nothing like Francesca, Sam can't help thinking, the pain beneath her ribcage growing more acute.

'I'm sure we're all looking forward to getting to know Julian and Beth.' Her father smiles warmly from the couple to the congregation. 'I ask you to keep them in your prayers over the coming weeks. We hope their move will go smoothly and they'll quickly feel at home here among their new family.'

There are calls of 'Amen", 'Praise the Lord!', 'God bless you,' from around the museum hall.

Her father puts his arm around Julian's shoulders, drawing him close to the microphone. 'I've asked our new brother if he would kindly give us the message this morning.'

'Thank you, Pastor Loveday.' Julian's smile takes on a more serious edge. 'It's truly wonderful to be with you here today.' He places his Bible on the lectern, his expression solemn as he finds his page and his wife and the pastor take their seats on the front row.

Her eyes move along the stage to Joe, seated with the musicians beside Lucy Longthorn. She hadn't felt anything when she'd heard they were going out together, just a sense of relief that he wouldn't be turning up on his motorbike anymore. But then, she'd made the mistake in thinking he must surely understand how different everything is, how nothing means the same as it had done before.

'D'you find it upsetting going to the meetings now?' she'd asked him. They were squashed together in the back of Ben's MG on the way to the youth group's first football match, against Yeovil

Community Church.
　　He'd rolled his eyes. 'What're you on about?'
　　'Do you still believe?' she'd pushed him.
　　He'd looked at her as though she was completely mad.
　'I'd like to begin by reading a passage from the book of John that I'm sure you all will have heard before.' Julian reads slowly, emphasising each word: 'I am the good shepherd, who is willing to die for the sheep. My sheep listen to my voice; I know them and they follow me.'